1

Also by Victoria Heckman

In the Coconut Man Series:
Kapu-Sacred
Kahuna-Priest

In the K.O.'d in Hawaii Series:
K.O.'d in Honolulu
K.O.'d in the Volcano
K.O.'d in the Rift
K.O.'d at Banzai Pipeline

In the Elizabeth Murphy Animal Communicator
Series:
Burn Out
Wet Work

Stand Alone Mysteries:
Pearl Harbor Blues

Kahuna

Priest

A Coconut Man Mystery of Ancient Hawai`i

Victoria Heckman

2017 Revenge Publishing

Published in the United States by Revenge Publishing.

ISBN: 978-0-9970880-2-1

Cover Design: Liam Heckman
Author Photo: Blue Moon Photography

This is a work of fiction. Because I have set the series before European contact, there was freedom as well as difficulty in its creation. I have intentionally not named a specific date or island. I also created my own ahupua`a, or village, and use those words interchangeably, although they are not truly the same in definition.

Ritual and prayer was the framework of Hawaiian life upon which all activities were built, so that is woven throughout. The rituals have been modified to maintain their sanctity, but the proper principles have been included.

Some aspects of the life or culture have been altered, such as the strict eating rules because of lack of written information. The basis of this book is oral tradition, which was later transcribed. That information is difficult to get and transcriptions and translations vary. Another reason is to continue the fictional plot. I have also amended the families of gods and goddesses for the story. Things may not have happened this way, but they could have, and that is the premise of any story. Aloha and mahalo!

Acknowledgements

As always I want to thank my family for their support. My editor, Sue McGinty, and the support of Sisters in Crime-Central Coast Chapter.

He hōʻike na ka pō

A revelation of the night.

Chapter One

Coconut Man adjusted a frond hat of his own design more securely to block the sun. He strode confidently away from the village, his home for the last season. He bore the fruits of much labor in the form of hats and baskets, samples he hoped to sell or trade in a village to the southeast. He had not been there on his travels yet but had heard the people were prosperous and welcoming.

Most Hawai'ians did not travel a great deal, but he was a wandering spirit and had spent much of his remembered life afoot. This recent stay in this village was the longest he'd remained in one place. He had learned many things, had new acquaintances and made promises to return. The most important one to a little boy called Kaleo. So named 'the voice' for his strident birth cries, made more appropriate by his loud and boisterous nature as he grew older. Coconut Man smiled at the memory of Kaleo's round brown cheeks puffed in concentration or split in a smile. Thoughts drifted to Kaleo's lovely widowed mother, Lele, with whom he'd found unexpected kinship and companionship. And perhaps, something else? He would return to her village after his excursion to the south village. After all, he had promised.

The sun warmed the trail and the increased slope in the terrain stretched his muscles. Traveling again felt good. His water gourd slapped gently against his back and the weight of fruit and dried fish comforted him, as did his hand-woven treasures. He had learned to dye the fronds at the last village and he had added many beautiful things to his work: shells, dried flowers and fruit, feathers. As he thought of each thing, he noticed that attached to it was a person. *Interesting. That had not happened before.* For example, the fisherman Io had taught him to use dye, the way he dyed his nets dark to hide them from the fish. *Lele, the kapa cloth maker*—here a warm glow suffused him and he quickly glanced up to see if anyone noticed. Of course, no one did. He was on a high trail crossing the flank of a smoking mountain. Hotter and drier here, with fewer trees and no water, he was glad he had listened to Tutu. She was the village elder and a healing *kahuna,* who told him it would be high and hot for several days as he crossed the wasteland.

He went back to his thoughts of Lele as the sky, white from heat except for a plume of smoke, pressed down. He drank from his gourd and rested under a scrawny 'ohi'a tree. He crunched a mountain apple with his strong teeth and tried to calculate where he was. He had walked almost a whole day. The sun god La sank in the sky toward the ocean, signaling the end of his day. Coconut Man creaked a little as he stood. He was not as young as he once was. Unmarried and childless, he thought it would always be so until he had met his new little *'ohana*—family—at the last village.

As far as he could see were stunted trees and black rock. He knew he was nearing the home of Pele, goddess of the volcano, and although he prayed regularly to all the gods and goddesses, he hadn't given much thought to Pele since she lived so far. Now, seeing the bleakness, feeling isolated in the coming dusk, he thought, perhaps, he had been hasty in his decision to pass through her lands. He had not prayed to her, asked permission, nor even spoken to Tutu about it.

Tutu knew he was coming here! And she said nothing. What did that mean? A breeze brought a chill and he shivered in his *malo.* The loincloth was short and perfect for hot days. Now, he pulled out a length of *kapa* cloth and wrapped his shoulders. A little better. He continued on the trail, not knowing where else to go. Flatness in a sense, yet waves of lava and boulders stretched into the distance, none of it inviting him to step off and find shelter. Too far from the beach, so no coconut trees to build a frond lean-to. He sighed in frustration. Finally, it grew too dark to continue and he carefully worked his way off the trail a bit, trying to stay on the smooth *pāhoehoe* lava and avoid the sharp *a'a*. A cut foot would not help him get to the next village. And how would he run if he needed? Now why did he think of that? Run? Impossible on the lava. He saw a dark shape, denser than the surrounding black and froze. Nothing moved, no sound greeted him.

He carefully stepped forward and found the darkness of a shallow cave. Relief flooded him and he curled his body into the rock. Surprisingly warm, he ate some of his fish. He decided to leave some food and water for tomorrow. He might have trouble finding more. Didn't Tutu mention a fresh stream? He dozed a little while he tried to recollect what she said. From his den, he saw a slice of night sky and welcomed the stars as his guardians. Comforted, he fell into an exhausted sleep.

Unsure what woke him, Coconut Man, eyes still closed, listened. Footsteps near. Low voices. The smell of a torch, smoky, burning.

Happy to have found company, he opened his eyes. The stars were blocked by a shape. A shape made of two shapes. Two men in a struggle. Afraid to move, he remained still, holding his breath in his cave. The struggle became violent. One of the figures made choking sounds and the smell of his fear drifted to Coconut Man.

A grunt of effort and something warm splashed onto Coconut Man. Paralyzed, he remained still. As one figure dragged the other away, he closed his eyes and prayed to Pele for help. None came.

Chapter Two

Coconut Man awoke from his dream. Someone had been attacked. *That's what I get for traveling alone without proper directions*, he scolded himself. He stretched one leg at a time out of his shallow shelter and decided to make fresh water his priority once he got back on the trail.

He rolled out of the cave on hands and knees and faced a dark, sticky pool. Icy water rolled down his back as he understood his dream was a reality. Cautiously, he poked his head up and stood, glancing side to side. No one and nothing. Just like yesterday. Except a lot of blood and it was still wet. No blood beyond a few feet. Fortunately, the trail was near. He repositioned his *kapa* cloak and walked rapidly in the dawn.

The sun god La began his journey across the sky and the day warmed. Coconut Man reached the peak of the trail, mid-way up the mountain. The white smoke continued to rise, and as he headed on the downhill side, saw more smoke near the ocean. He finished his fish and remaining water and fruit, too afraid to step off the trail again.

Was it odd he'd met no one? No hunters, no sign of anyone, besides those last night. Because of the volcano, he knew the traditional cone shape of the *ahupua'a*—that tract of land that begins high in the mountains and widens as it reaches the sea—might not apply. Tall at the top and fat at the bottom, like a slice of fruit. Now he was really hungry. What kind of village would be here?

Another thing he hadn't asked Tutu. How did she know so much? Women didn't travel much. But they did talk a lot. And she was a *kahuna*, a healer priest.

He folded his *kapa* and stuffed it back into his carrier pouch. Thirsty. He saw green in the distance. Forest and now, instead of smoke, he encountered wisps of mist. Decidedly cooler. The trail branched occasionally and he took a side path downhill looking for water. He hoped the muddy track meant a stream. Instead, the mist grew heavier and a light rain fell. Grumpily pulling on the *kapa,* he heard the rush of water over the whisper of rain in the giant ferns.

The slope was definite now and he hurried to the source. A narrow, fast-moving stream bubbled cheerfully at his feet. He knelt and drank deeply, then filled his calabash. The gourd was comfortingly heavy when he rose and surveyed the area. Forest towered on both sides of the stream, but sparse enough that he could move along the banks. A thin layer of rich soil covered the lava while fruit trees and giant ferns nestled amonth the taller, mist-laden trunks.

This must be where Tutu meant. A village needs water, so uphill or down, it should be close. Down would take him perhaps toward the sea, so down he went. An *ahupua'a* needed all kinds of land and resources: uplands, lowlands, fresh water, ocean, terraces, and gardens. He felt he was heading in the right direction.

He noted small fish in the stream. A good sign, but he had no means to catch them, so he continued pulling off fruit as he went. Some he ate, and some he saved for later.

Bright light indicated an opening in the forest. What he saw astonished him. The trees just stopped. A vast expanse of dried lava spread as far as he could see. A few 'ohi'a trees struggled out of the blackness. His choice was to return to the forest or cross the dry lake. It was against his nature to go back. Tentatively he stepped up onto the plain of lava. Thankfully it was mainly *pāhoehoe*—

smooth and whorled, warm and easy on bare feet.

Oppressive heat on the lava field and he told himself it was because he was walking downhill on sun-warmed black rock. He tried not to let in images of the crust beneath his feet collapsing and dropping him into vast pools of fire to a horrible death. He drank from his calabash and hoped for another stream, however unlikely that seemed now. He turned and looked back the way he'd come. No sign of the forest. As though it had vanished. Unsettling. Because he had walked down the mountain and the piles of lava obscured the trees, he felt insignificant and alone.

La was nearly straight above him when he reached one end of the lava field. He had come to a dropoff at the edge of the sea. A bit farther down he saw where fire spilled into the ocean, steam billowed skyward, and the smell of something burning, but worse than he'd ever smelled, rushed to his nostrils.

Pele was making land. As he stood here, at the edge of the world it felt, she created more earth for her people. It was truly awe-inspiring. And terrifying. What if she saw him? What if she dropped him into the ocean because he was breaking some *kapu* he didn't know? So many things were sacred and only chiefs, *ali'i,* had access to them. What if this was one of them? He'd never heard of it, but. . . he quickly backed away from the edge and began to make his way across the lava again, paralleling the shore, back far enough so he felt safer. He mumbled a prayer to Pele for forgiveness and thanks.

His feet grew very warm in places and he finally saw why. Slits in the lava opened to show bright orange rivers, like the rays of La, streaming beneath him. Heat and smell pulsed from them and he soon learned to listen to his feet as they warmed. He was getting close to another sunbeam in the earth.

This made for a much longer journey and he kept his head down, careful of a slip or a hole. He had run out of water and fruit again as La made his way lower and lower into the ocean behind him. Coconut Man noticed his feet had not felt warm for some time and he stopped and stretched his overtaxed ankles. Walking on lava was hard work. He saw tree tops in the distance and his heart lifted as he thought he might finally step off this bleak wilderness.

La was dipping a toe into the ocean when Coconut Man gratefully climbed down a tumbled slope of lava rock to flat forest floor. Walking here would be such a welcome relief! The familiar smell of rotting fruit comforted him as he searched for something to eat. The forest had its own way of working, one he was completely at home with.

As he walked, he noted the plants seemed to be ordered—crops, perhaps? Now in complete dusk, he smelled cooking fires. He was near a village! His stomach rumbled in anticipation. He had not forgotten last night, however. Was it only last night? He cautiously approached the fires and noise; the happy babble of the evening activities.   He watched from behind a screen of jungle to be sure.

"Aloha," he called when he felt safe enough.   Several people stopped and turned to him in surprise. He stepped out so he would not alarm them. Especially warriors.

"Aloha," one called back hesitantly.

"I am alone. I've traveled quite a distance today and I am hungry. I have things to trade. May I join you?"

The women stayed near their tasks, but some of the men came forward to greet him. They were older, not the elders or infirm it seemed, but on closer inspection, Coconut Man saw no man of warrior age at all. That seemed strange, but his stomach commanded that he pay attention to its needs first.

Coconut Man was led to a mat near the fire.   This village was not as prosperous as the one he'd left. Not as many *hale* and those he saw were in need of repair. The food was plentiful and the people warm, so he set his concerns aside for the moment.

A silence fell over the village after the meal. Unlike his previous home, where there was still muted bustle after the evening repast, the group was quiet. The other village boasted *kōnane* games into the night. Large pocked boulders used as game boards were rolled out to much laughing and betting, derision and relaxing. Here, he barely heard the women putting the children to bed and no quiet chatter of the day's gossip.

The men around the eating mat gazed at him. Not with hostility, but caution and curiosity, perhaps? Unsure how to begin discussing his baskets in this odd atmosphere, he cleared his throat and checked each face. This would normally be the time where he would be given a sleeping mat, or perhaps a place in the men's sleeping *hale*, but no offer was forthcoming.

"Mahalo for sharing your meal with me," he began. The faces changed to concerned resignation. *What was going on here?* "I am Coconut Man and I weave baskets and hats of the finest quality. I travel village to village trading my wares." Silence. A few nods. A silent palpable wave of *'What do you want from us?'* swept over him.

Since he'd come to live in his 'home village' as he'd come to think of it, he had learned a great deal from Tutu. A *kahuna*—expert—she had taught him some of her numerous skills. She was a healer, but she had also shared some of her more specialized abilities, such as tuning into what others were thinking and feeling. He'd had no need of it for some time, but now the skill rose up in him unbidden. The villagers were terrified and wanted to hide it from him. To protect him? Themselves? He heard the pounding of their hearts, their stillness was not calmness, but fear, like a bird stills on a branch to avoid a predator. He was not a predator, but they did not know that.

Blood rushed through their veins, the women silenced the *kamali'i* in the *hale.* The men waited. For what? All he had said was he wanted to trade baskets, but they thought it was something more, perhaps.

"What is wrong?" he asked. "I am here to trade. Is that not acceptable?" Coconut Man took in the energy of the circle. He had learned to read *aka* lines from Tutu as well. Those lines of energy that stream from person to person like a spider's web during *ho'oponopono*—that time of setting things to right; problem-solving. Now the lines ran red and freely among them all, like the fingers of lava he'd seen racing to the ocean. Something was very wrong here.

He had never actually led a healing ceremony. He had participated and it had not ended well for him. He was afraid to try to help here. He noticed something else unheard of. This village had no *kahuna.* He sent out his consciousness and 'felt' around the village. Not just absent from this circle, but nowhere in the *ahupua'a* did he feel the energy of a healing or spiritual being. Usually a village had many *kāhuna*; healing, fishing, farming, each *kahuna* had a 'specialty' and he felt none of them; all he felt was a hole. He pressed further and felt great emptiness and fear. Something had happened to all the *kāhuna* here. He felt that many were also the warriors, guardians of the village. And they were all gone. No women of rank remained either.

He might be afraid to try to help here, but another fear struck him as far greater. What if no one tried? What if no one could help and he had been sent here and he did nothing? Perhaps Pele herself had sent him. Stranger things had happened. Tutu had taught him to leave his body. Nothing in his life had prepared him for that, either in need or in action. Now here was another situation he had been tossed into, like Kaleo tossed a twig into the Wai River to see what would happen.

The gods and goddess are funny. He glanced again at the circle of somber faces. Even the wind had stopped pushing the palms. Silence. He was about to speak when he felt a blackness drop on him, pressing against his skin, trying to get inside him. He felt this blackness was already inside the villagers; had taken, destroyed perhaps, the warriors, the *kāhuna*, anyone who could help. Without a direct thought, he cried out to Tutu. He understood she knew what was happening to him but could do nothing yet. It was up to him.

Suddenly he knew. Sorcery was at the heart of this village. Black magic had taken the people, the prosperity, the spirit. And he might be the only one to return it.

"Why do you say something is wrong?" asked an older but strong-looking man. His long hair was coming unbound and glistened in the firelight.

"I am Coconut Man," he said. Custom dictated that the others be named as well.

The man pointed to himself. "Kula." The others did not give their names. Coconut Man did not understand this caution; after all, they had fed him and that was a custom as well. *Who was he to find fault?* he thought. He didn't even know his 'real' name. He sighed.

"I am from a village two days walk from here. I came to trade, but now I see you may not need my wares." In fact, he had seen no baskets at all, but he wanted them to talk to him. "Who is your weaver?"

Kula looked at the eldest at the fire and nodded. The elder shifted to a more comfortable position and began to speak.

"I am Moho. Headman. For now." His eyes slid to Kula and then to the others.

"Are you the weaver?" Coconut Man thought this was probably a ridiculous question because the village headman had more important things to do than weave, but he was at a loss on how to proceed. They were afraid of something.

"No. I am in charge here." Silence again.

Coconut Man looked at the circle of stunned faces around the fire. "I know what is happening here," he told them. "I am here to help." He thrust his energy along all the red *aka* lines. They lessened in intensity but remained scarlet. He tried again and spread his power like a *kapa* over the whole web instead of running it along just the lines. The lines turned pink and pulsed less.

As if waking from a deep sleep, the people blinked and moved, their gazes becoming seeing, instead of just facing him. He took a deep breath, determined to help.

the women crept from their *hale* and sat outside the men's circle, still and silent. He decided to be bold.

"You have no *kāhuna*. None at all." He glanced around the circle at the startled faces. "Why?"

"You are a *kahuna*?" Kula asked. When he turned his body, Coconut Man saw a long scar down his leg, jagged and deep, the tissue twisted and ropey like pāhoehoe lava. That explained why he was not gone waging some war, or wherever the rest of the able-bodied were.

"I have some training. Enough to know something is very wrong here. Can you tell me what has happened?"

The men shook their heads. "We cannot," Moho whispered. "Our keiki, our wāhine. . . the rest of us. We would be gone."

The pressure Coconut Man felt increased. A clap of thunder and a bolt of lightning split the sky. The spell was broken. As fat drops fell, the fire was banked and everyone scattered to various hāle. Moho beckoned Coconut Man to the single men's sleeping hale.

As Coconut Man began his thanks, Moho put his hand over his own mouth. *No more talk.*

Chapter Three

The men's sleeping *hale* was quiet. The men shifted position on their mats, but he heard no snoring. They lay still and silent. He wondered if they actually slept. It was too dark inside to see their faces, so if they lay with eyes open watching him he had no way of knowing. *Why did I think of that?* Now he felt like all eyes were on him. He was tired from his day's walk and the strained conversation around the campfire. Not to mention the death the night before. He assumed it was a death, but he couldn't be sure.

His discomfort increased until he could no longer lie on his mat. He knew he would not sleep and he needed rest. He crept from the *hale* and made his way into the jungle, staying far from well-traveled paths. Outside of the *hale,* the moon made it possible to find his way. When he felt far enough away from the village for comfort, he made a nest and wrapped himself in his *kapa* and finally slept.

La was just making his way out of the sea when Coconut Man crept back into the village. He watched for a moment from the jungle, but all was quiet. Slowly people awoke and began their chores. He returned to the fire circle of last night. He had left his baskets here, those he brought for trade. Damp with dew, but untouched. That surprised him a little. The energy in the village was strange, sinister even, but at least they were not thieves. He smiled a little at this. He would try again to help them. They did not mention anyone missing from their ranks. The man he thought had been killed; would they have spoken of him? Perhaps he was not from this village.

Kula found him musing on a stone near the fire pit. "Aloha." Kula limped toward him at a good clip.

"Aloha." Coconut Man smiled.

"Perhaps you could join us and trade some of your baskets?"

"Of course." Coconut Man was instantly wary. All the man's fear and hesitancy of last night was absent. "Where should I display them?"

"I will show you the best place. Have you eaten?"

"Not yet." Coconut Man's stomach rumbled in response.

"Come to the eating *hale* in a little while and we will eat," Kula said.

Coconut Man nodded and Kula hobbled off. *He moves quickly and efficiently for someone who walks like a canoe rolls in the surf*, Coconut Man mused. *And silently.*

In the eating *hale*, much laughing and talking ensued. Coconut Man was welcomed and given food, but an unseen tension, some falseness pulsed within. He sat next to Kula and another man.

"Is this everyone?" he asked the man, whose name he learned was Liloa.

"Yes, yes. Everyone is here. Who would miss a meal?" He slapped Coconut Man on the shoulder. His laugh sounded forced.

Coconut Man ate slowly, eyes roving the faces around him. He did not know of the women, he had seen only glimpses of their faces outside the fire's glow last night. But yes, he was sure of it. A man was missing. He didn't get a name last night. An older man who hadn't contributed much to the discussion was not in the *hale*.

"Liloa? Where is that other man? Last night he sat next to you, but I don't see him here."

Liloa stopped chewing. Thoughts raced across his face although he tried to mask his discomfort. "Oh, I am sure he is about somewhere."

"Who is it?"

"'Oloa. He is fine. Just morning business." The heavy heat had not yet come to the village, so the mist of sweat on his upper lip said Liloa was lying.

"I can help. Tell me what is wrong." Coconut Man's thoughts flashed to the night on the lava field. "Has he been taken by someone? Why?"

Liloa dropped his fruit back onto the mat. "You are the gnat, the fly that will not go away," he whispered with resignation, not anger. "It was foretold you would come. We did not believe it was you when you arrived last night. You are so . . . plain."

"Foretold? Who foretold? I am not plain. I am not young, though," Coconut Man said indignantly. "I did not know I was coming here. How did someone foretell it? And you have no *kahuna* to foretell anything."

Liloa looked around the *hale*. "Not here. I believe you. Meet me by the trail to the sea after the meal. I know Kula is

37

letting you show your wares in the village. He hopes to distract you until you leave. There is danger here. 'Oloa is gone. He will be sacrificed, I think. It is too late for him, but perhaps not for the rest of us." Liloa drank deeply from a calabash, rose abruptly and disappeared through a rustle of pili grass door curtain.

The hum of feigned conversation continued but Coconut Man pretended not to notice the eyes on him, the calculation and speculation that accompanied the stares.

He also rose and left to find Kula and display his wares *for no real reason*, he thought. *Well, saving someone, or many someones, in this village is a real reason. Even if they don't want me to.*

Kula met him in the middle of the village with a hearty wave. "Here, here is a mat for you. I have already told everyone you would be here and to trade with you right away. If they want the best choice, that is." Kula's smiled a shark's grin.

So I can be on my way as soon as possible, Coconut Man filled in. "I can stay as long as necessary," he said evenly. "People can tell me what they want and I can weave it for them. There is no rush." As Kula seemed about to interrupt, he continued, "I even add special things so the hats and baskets can be different: shells, flowers. I am working on dyeing the fronds, too. Like a fishing net."

Kula's eyes squared a little at the top. He was not pleased. However, he smiled again and said, "That is wonderful. And unique. I can tell we have no one here as skilled as you in this trade. Your talent will be welcome."

I am willing to bet otherwise, thought Coconut Man. He smiled hugely, too. "And no need for any special accommodations. I take my *kapa* and sleep where the winds blow me. I am happy to trade for food or other items, so no one need be put out by my visit." *That way no one can kidnap me in my sleep. Ha.*

Kula nodded and turned away, heading toward the trail to the beach. Coconut Man sobered. *This is not a game. Perhaps it was not wise to engage Kula openly. Now he knows I will distance myself at night. I thought I was so clever. But now I have also told him I am alone and can be easily stolen away.* He sighed. *Clever Coconut Man is lōlō.* Stupid.

Before he set out his items, he decided to meet Liloa. He followed Kula's steps and after the main clearing, he found several well-traveled paths leaving the village. Unsure which led to the beach, he went straight, as the others seemed to parallel the shore through the jungle. However, he thought it might be a good idea to explore those paths before he needed them.

After a few minutes' walk in which the temperature rose considerably, the forest thinned to nothing and a plain of grainy beach stretched underfoot. No sign of Liloa. Perhaps this was not the right beach from the right path. *Well, Liloa should have said if there was more than one way.*

He stepped ankle-deep into the water and its chill felt wonderful. He was reluctant to go in deeper as this was an unfamiliar beach. At his old village, he had overcome his fear of the ocean, somewhat. There, the beach and water were known to him. He knew the royal fishpond, the coral reef and a perfect swimming spot for the *keiki,* which is where he preferred to wade, if he had to go in at all. He was still not very happy in the water. In the Wai River, he used to bathe every morning. Refreshing, flowing past the village, but not too quickly, it was a time of cleansing and clearing of the body and mind. Ocean water held frightening creatures. He was not a fisherman and only ate what he caught from the shore or tide pools, or what was given to him. He'd had an unfortunate incident in the ocean and knew he *could* swim, but that he did not like to. He had also learned that *honu*, sea turtle, was his *aumakua* or family god. But again, he wished he hadn't had to learn it quite that way.

He wandered down the beach, in water no deeper than his knees, looking for shells to adorn his baskets.

A shout brought his head up. Liloa charged out of the jungle onto the beach.

"I'm sorry, Coconut Man. I was waiting for you, but Kula came and I had to avoid him. I ended up ahead of him on the trail until finally, he turned toward the uplands. He does not farm *kalo,* so I don't know where he was going. I thought he knew I was there and was, I don't know, hunting me."

"Why would you think he is hunting you?"

"I don't know. Maybe he knew I was meeting you?"

"Is he a hunter?" Liloa nodded. "Perhaps he was going hunting?"

"Yes, yes. That is probably it. He did have his spear. That must be it." Liloa's breath finally slowed.   "What are you doing?"

"I was looking for shells while I waited for you." He showed his finds. "I put them on my hats and baskets. Would you like me to make you one?"

"Yes, that would be wonderful.   I farm in the uplands and I would like a nice, big hat." Liloa's smile split his brown face.

"I have to get back to display my wares, so what did you want to tell me?"

Liloa glanced up and down the beach. "Let's sit in the shade. Harder for someone to see us."

In the morning light, a handful of shells in a fold of his *malo*, his feet sticky from sea and sand, it was hard for Coconut Man to recapture the fear of the night before. Maybe he was exaggerating the events? Maybe this was the way the village protected itself from invading *ali'i*? He had been through a territorial war himself last season. Frightening and life-changing, he had helped the women and children to safety in *mauka*—mountain—caves. Then he had been in the thick of the battle. He shook his head. Liloa had seated himself with his back against a sturdy palm and had already begun his story.

"Wait." Coconut Man held up his hand. "Please start again. I was not ready." He sat against a neighboring palm and nodded; raising his eyebrows for, *yes, go on.*

"I am telling you this," Liloa began, "in case I disappear, too. I want someone to tell my story. So many have gone." He fell silent.

Several moments passed while Liloa's story moved silently across his face. His lips pinched and his eyes glistened.

"I know this is hard," Coconut Man said, "but I can only help if you tell me what has happened. Why has no one heard of this?"

News did travel between villages and even among islands. Battles between chiefs, difficulties with crops or fishing grounds, it all made its way around.

"We are too afraid to tell. At first, we sent a runner to say there was trouble in the village. He did not return, and later we found his *malo* and spear. There were other things: his hair had been cut off. Most of it was left in a pile, but some had been burned. There was much blood. You know what that means?"

Coconut Man was not sure, although it did not sound good after his own experience. He shook his head.

"Magic of some kind. Black magic."

"You can find the *kahuna* doing that, can't you? And what makes you think it is sorcery? '*Ana 'ana* doesn't have to be evil. Perhaps you misunderstood?"

"Then why did the runner, Kou, never return? Why was there blood and hair? You know we protect those things. They can be used against you. Your nail parings, you bury those, don't you?" Liloa didn't wait for an answer. "Of course you do!"

Coconut Man glanced at his own very short nails. Climbing trees for fruit and fronds to weave kept his nails this way. But he did know. Babies' birth cords were always taken away and buried secretly so they could not be used to curse the baby or the family. Hair and nail trimmings were *kapu*—sacred and hidden. If the wrong person or *kahuna* found them, they were powerful talismans to be used against someone. That was common knowledge. But this . . . this seemed worse.

Liloa was still talking. "Kou was just the first. More disappeared after that. We did have *kāhuna*. Of course we did. But they went. One by one. At first, we thought perhaps, an illness, and in some cases, old age. But it was very particular. Then the old headman sent out a group of warriors to search. They did not return. The village was very afraid. The last *kahuna* told us she thought we had offended the gods somehow. We live on Pele's land, so perhaps she was angry with us. Some of us, farming the uplands had seen an old woman in the *kalo* patch. Then another group saw a beautiful young woman, a stranger, sitting by the fishpond. Later, when a hunting party followed a boar onto the lava, they saw a white dog running across the rock." Liloa's eyes were huge. "Pele," he whispered.

Coconut Man felt a shiver tickle his spine. "What happened next?"

"We thought Pele was telling us she was angry. We made fresh offerings to her. We danced, we chanted, but nothing seemed to help. More people disappeared. This darkness, you feel it too, don't you?" Coconut Man nodded. "It settled over the village. It is not as bad during the day, but at night, it is a hat on our *ahupua'a* and we wait to see who the darkness takes next."

"Why is it taking people? It doesn't make sense if to invade a village one person at a time, then you will have no one to rule?"

"We don't know. It doesn't happen every night. Or even every moon. We cannot say. It is happening more often, now, though. Nāwai was taken just before you came. And now 'Oloa last night."

Coconut Man supposed Nāwai might have been the man on the lava flow. Since he hadn't seen him, he could not even describe him to Liloa. To mention him or not? Perhaps not right now.

"Who would do this?" Coconut Man asked. "For what purpose?"

"We don't know. Kula took over as *konohiki*—overseer—of the village when the first headman disappeared. What I can tell you is that all of our most powerful and brave people are being taken. Our warriors, our *kāhuna,* our leaders. We are afraid and darting about like food fish in the royal fishpond. We are trapped. We have short, whispered meetings because we don't know who is watching. We barely trust each other. When the last *kahuna* said help would come from far away and from a strange place at that, we didn't know what to think. Then she disappeared and we can't ask her for more. We hoped for a chief's visit we hadn't heard about. A surprise visit. He does that sometimes. But now," Liloa's gaze was half speculating, half pleading. "Now, I think it is you."

Chapter Four

"Me?" Coconut Man said. "You think it's me? I am help sent by the gods?"

"Well, yes," Liloa said. "It does seem unlikely."

Coconut Man tried not to take offense, even though a moment ago he had agreed with Liloa. He was not young. He was not a warrior, or of any special background. Tutu had taught him a few things, but he was not equipped to go up against the volcano goddess by any stretch. He made baskets of unequaled complexity and loveliness, but he would not fend off a curse or a spear with a basket, no matter how well crafted.

"Which gods? If you think it is Pele you have offended, who would send me to contest her?" Coconut Man asked.

"We do not know. Her sister perhaps? Na-maka-o-ka-ha'i?"

"The sea goddess?"

"It is well known that they did not get along. She was always drenching Pele's fires with her waves. So much so that Pele had to change homes and come here."

"Why would Pele take your people?"

"We don't know! And now we have no one to ask. Only you." Liloa sounded accusing.

"I said I would help. I will do my best. But Pele . . ." he trailed off and thought. "Has Pele taken any of your people? I mean her lava. Has she destroyed any villages?"

"No. Not that we have heard. Nothing from our village has been damaged." Liloa tapped his chin in thought. "Nothing even close."

"Well, that doesn't sound like Pele. When she is angry, everyone knows it."

"Why do we keep seeing her then? Why do people disappear after she has been seen?"

"I don't know. I will try to find out." Coconut Man brushed the sand from his hands. "I must go. I have to pretend, at least, to trade my wares. I can weave baskets and hats and perhaps find out more from those who trade." He rose and headed back the way he'd come. He glanced back to see Liloa still seated, slumped in defeat.

Coconut Man spread the mat Kula had provided and placed his hats and baskets in a pleasing display. He pulled the shells and rocks out of his *malo* and turned them in his gnarled hands as he waited for customers. People seemed wary of approaching him, but since all he did was sit in the shade and practice weaving his new treasures into frond blossoms and tiny baskets, he did not appear threatening. He found a way to weave a tiny basket with a lid and place a shell inside, like a secret present. *There. That looked lovely.*

A shadow fell over his mat. He glanced up and a woman with a toddler clinging to her leg watched him.

"Aloha," he greeted her.

"Aloha." She took a deep breath. "Your wares are lovely. I have dried eel and *kalo*. May I trade for a basket?" she asked shyly.

Not wanting to scare her off he asked, "Which one were you interested in?"

She pointed to a large, sturdy basket for storing *kapa* and other bulky items. It was worth rather more than dried eel and *kalo*, but perhaps she had information.

"Yes, I think I can do that. However, I will make you one. These are for everyone to see and I will make each person what is asked for."

She smiled and picked up the child, balancing it on a hip. All Coconut Man saw of its face were two large, brown eyes under a curtain of hair, split by fingers he

53

assumed were in the mouth. He could not tell boy or girl. When *keiki* were so small, it was hard for him to tell.

To put the woman at ease, he quickly wove a bird on a thin stem of frond and handed the bouncing toy to the child. It squealed with delight and wanted down to play with it. She obliged and as she continued to peruse his stock he said, "I understand there is some concern in the village? I saw 'Oloa was missing this morning?"

Her eyes welled up. *Oh, no,* he thought. *I have a gift for saying the wrong thing.*

"I'm sorry. I didn't mean to upset you."

"He is my brother-in-law. My husband is also gone. Earlier." She glanced around the clearing, but no one was near. "He is a warrior. He was following the *kahuna*'s guidance. He was sent out to discover what is happening to our people."

"I'm so sorry." He suddenly wondered why she was opening up to him.

"I was told you were coming. He, my husband, told me. The *kahuna* told him you would help." She glanced at him. "I did not expect you to be so . . . ordinary."

This was becoming a pattern. "It is my disguise," he said a little testily. "Who would feel fear from me?"

"That is true." She squatted down to see the hats. She kept her head low. "I will tell you more of what my husband told me. He felt he would be taken. I think he wanted to be taken."

"What? Who would want that?"

She tried on a hat. "Many in the village think Pele is angry with us. But, she is not. She is our family god and I would know. She is trying to help us. Someone is not only after us, but after her as well."

"Can't Pele look after herself? She is a goddess, and one of the most powerful."

The woman placed the hat back on the mat. Aloud she said, "I would like a

55

hat as well." She picked up her child. "I will meet you to discuss my basket and hat." Then she whispered, "I will tell you all I know. Watch out for Kula. He may be dangerous."

They both glanced up to see Kula and another villager coming toward the display. "Don't tell anyone until we can talk again. I am Pua. And this is Hiwahiwa." The child swung her bird toy and echoed, "Heeeva heeeva!"

Ah. A daughter. Precious One. That made sense. She was lovely and quiet. Unlike his friend, Kaleo, The Voice. He smiled as he thought of Kaleo and the other children of his village. Naturally, his thoughts drifted to Kaleo's mother, Lele. He was missing them. That life. He realized he would be glad to return when this was over. Perhaps his wandering days were growing to a close. An interesting thought.

Kula and a woman had reached Coconut Man's wares. "Here. I have brought Lehua. She would like a basket. She said," Kula said brusquely.

"I said I would like to see them, Kula." Lehua spoke firmly.

"We want him to sell all his baskets so he knows we are a prosperous village of welcoming people," Kula said.

"What I am doing," Coconut Man began, "is showing everyone what choices I have, and then I will make them. I am keeping these for looking. Not for buying." He eyed Kula.

Two things struck Coconut Man. One, that Kula was a poor listener. And two, that he was very pushy and demanding, acting more like a village headman than the actual village headman, Moho. A chill trickled down his back in the heat. Perhaps that did not bode well for Moho. *Maybe Kula wants to be headman. After all, wasn't Moho konohiki only because the other one was taken?*

Once Lehua got down to the business of negotiating for a basket, Kula wandered off again. Coconut Man struck a deal, but kept an eye out for Kula and anyone who seemed allied with him. It was difficult to tell in this short time who was on what side. He did not like or trust Kula, but when he thought about it, did not have a clear reason. He did trust Pua, and again, for no clear reason. As Lehua concluded her business and left his mat, Tutu's words spilled as clearly into his mind as if she were whispering in his ear.

Wait. Wait to trust. Send out yourself tonight. Stay in the jungle to sleep. Look for Pele. She does need your help. Her enemies are powerful. I cannot help you the way I want to. My way is bound and I am a prisoner of my past.

Coconut Man shook himself alert as if from a daydream. He glanced up to see two men crossing the clearing carrying fish. A good catch. They noticed his glazed appearance and curved away from him. His reputation as the savior might be spreading. That was probably not a good thing. And spirit walking! Tutu wanted him to send himself out again. Where did she propose he go? He sighed. That was a risky thing and he was not good at it nor comfortable doing it.   If he was to be kidnapped, while he was 'walking' would be the perfect time. Fortunately, no one here knew he spirit walked. He hoped.

Chapter Five

La's chariot headed for the sea, and another day came to a close. Cook fires flared and delicious smells wafted on the breeze. Men returned from chores, children collected firewood and the day's bustle picked up again after the heat of the day. Coconut Man gathered his samples and the new baskets he had started, and tucked everything in a safe place for the night, far from where he might sleep. He decided to sleep in a different spot each night, but he didn't know where was safe in the village. He'd been to the sea on one path, but that one was popular and he didn't want to use it.

The other two in that direction were promising, but he'd slept *makai*—toward the sea—last night. Perhaps tonight he would try in the mountains—*mauka.*

After the meal, of course. He was hungry. But for now, he moved toward the upland *kalo* patch, just to see. He had time for a quick look before it was too dark. *Mealtimes were also great for listening,* he thought.

He grabbed a fallen mountain apple and crunched as he trotted uphill. It only seemed to increase his hunger, but he was sure that was only his imagination. After only a short way, he thought he had made a mistake coming out so late in the day and on an empty stomach. The path wended up among rocky outcrops, the footing slippery in the moist air. The uplands were good for farming but he had not thought to ask exactly where the *kalo* patch was. Foolishly, he'd thought the path would lead straight to it, but he realized he was lost.

I can just head back downhill and I will be at the village. Simple enough. He turned and carefully made his way down the slope, circling the biggest rocks and roots to save his feet in the dusk. He heard the trickle of a stream and his heart clenched. No stream accompanied him on the way up. He had taken a wrong turn and gone into another valley. He had no way of knowing which valley. He scolded himself. *Try to be so smart and now so stupid. Lo'lo'.*

No food, no *kapa*, no help. No one would look for him, but did he really want someone to? He truly did not know who to trust. He had started to trust Pua, but Tutu urged caution. He dropped into a squat to think. On the bright side, the likelihood of him being kidnapped from here was less now. He smiled grimly. *Not a lot of comfort.*

He continued down to the stream. Although it was getting cooler, his hike up the hill had made him thirsty. A stand of bananas brightened his prospects.

Although mostly green, they were tasty and a fallen fruit was sweet and ripe. He could barely see the sky through the dense trees now. Just over the stream shone a strip of star-filled night. Not enough to guide him, should he even know where he was, or where he wanted to go.

Navigating by *hoku,* star-travel, was another skill he lacked. Not a voyager of the sea and usually not a traveler by night, his need for knowledge of more than the basic stars had not arisen. In his nomadic basket trade, he ventured out during La's time, on well-worn travel paths between villages, not creeping about forests in the dark. By the time La's chariot had finished for the day, he was either in the next village or tucked up in a *kapa*, safe for the night. Of course, he avoided all paths with the Night Marchers, those hungry ghosts of warriors past, and any route that was known to have robbers. Even the northern paths reputed to have cannibals at times, he avoided just on rumor. He had never been one to take chances. *Or he had never been quite so stupid,* he amended. The *mai'a* leaves were large and he quickly stitched a few together with a stripped palm frond, his thumbnail, and sap for glue. *Not a bad* little *kapa,* he thought. He couldn't wrap it tightly around himself or the leaves would split, but it kept off the damp and smelled deliciously of banana. He carried his covering as he searched for a suitable sleeping place.

He knew hunger would again be upon him and so kept a somewhat futile watch for food. The moon rose and visibility improved, but he was still afraid to venture far. One of the bananas he'd eaten was green and was not settling well. He wanted to curl up. A tumble of rocks near the stream created an appropriate shelter. The rocks had chilled without the sun, but he felt safer with them at his back. He lay on his side and watched the stream bubble by. He wondered if he could sleep with the noise but decided it was a fine accompaniment and would cover his snores, should he be fortunate enough to sleep. A moment later another thought entered. He would not be able to hear anyone else approach him. He could not be seen from his side of the stream, but his shelter was a shallow hollow and visible from across the water. He could not win.

At this point, he closed his eyes and prayed to the gods for help. He chanted his quiet *mele*, entreating them to assist. A fleeting thought: *what if the god who hunts Pele hears me? One who is more powerful than Pele is to be feared.* He let that go. He relaxed and asked Tutu for help. He did not know his ancestors; he was one of a few unique persons who was unaware of his roots. A little disconcerting at times like this. One asked for help from all the spirit guides, *aumakua*, and ancestors in dealing with a problem. He always had to leave out that part. However, he treated the other village as his home now, and they, and their ancestors would have to do. He smiled thinking of explaining his request for their help.

Tutu appeared in his mind, and she was not amused. *If you are finished, you need to go.*

Tutu, in his visions, always appeared as a giant head. He did not know why that was so, but it was effective in getting him to pay attention. In life, Tutu was a small, wrinkled lady, motherly, in fact, who tottered about the home village making herbal cures and poultices for those ailing from illness or injury. In the spirit world, she was a giant, powerful being with many attributes, who chose to appear to him as a floating head. He wondered what she really looked like in spirit form, then decided perhaps it was best he not know.

Are you finished now? she asked.

Yes. He startled out of his physical body and rose above, looking down at his prone form, curled under its banana leaf. *I look tired.*

I'm sorry about that, but you have a task, Tutu said.

He could not see his spirit self, but it felt as real as his body below. *It does not hurt, however, and I am not hungry*, he mused.

Will you pay attention! Tutu screeched, out of patience.

Yes, yes. I am sorry. It has been a long time since I have done this. Why are you here? You said you could not help me.

I cannot go past the boundaries of the ahupua‘a.

Can you help me get back to the village?

No. Not now. You must stop what is happening. Dark magic is abroad. It has been building and I see that if this village falls, the island will fall.

Why did you wait so long? he asked petulantly.

It was not up to me. In truth, many things happen without my knowledge or consent. Problems resolve as often as they don't, and most do not need intervention. But this . . . this is more. The gods are involved this time, and although they do not like when man interferes, it has come to a state where they are also beginning to take sides. If the balance is upset, the people will pay the price. We are but instruments of the gods and while we honor them and pay them tribute, they think they do not need us.

If they don't need us, what can we do? Will they accept us?

Yes. Your new friend Pua was correct. Pele is in trouble. This is her land, but not hers alone. She has angered many over the years and now she needs our help.

What happened? How can a goddess, and Pele of all goddesses, be harmed?

Alliances were made. Sacrifices were given and taken. Those of us watching did not think it would come to this. This village is on the edge of disaster.

How am I supposed to help? I am not kahuna like you. I have no special powers.

Ah, but you do. Because you are man born of no woman, and because you are a new spirit, you have gifts. I will teach you, but there is no time now. You must go, and trust my words.

So, I am supposed to weave a basket and save the island? Save Pele with a basket that she could burn to cinder in a blink?

Something like that. Tutu sighed. *I feel myself pulling away. You will have to trust me and yourself. I may not be able to come to you again until this is over. However it ends.*

Wait! What do you mean; 'I am not born of woman'? You are frightening me, Tutu. What kind of new spirit am I?

Tutu had vanished. He still floated above his resting body, but he felt the cold and isolation now. Fear was foremost in his thoughts, but he remembered the hope Pua had when she met him. How she was willing to risk discovery on a tale of his coming to save them. The child, Hiwahiwa, deserved her mother, and even

69

her brave father, if he was still alive and Coconut Man could save him. He did not forget that his own village's future rested on the safety of this *ahupua'a.* Safety, it seemed, that only he could provide.

He closed his spirit eyes, took a deep breath and exhaled, the *aka* lines revealing the direction he needed to go.

Chapter Six

Coconut Man traveled the *aka* lines up and over the ridge. His body lay in the next valley over from the village. *Easy for when I return*, he thought. Even if he had not been able to see the energy lines glow bright red, he could feel them pulse, high and hot, and when he relaxed into the rhythm, they pulled him along. He floated, rushed even, above the earth. Although he moved his legs as if walking and then running, they never touched the ground. He knew his spirit-travel was from his mind, so he stopped moving his body, to see what would happen. He slowed. He pushed his mind forward, and the spirit travel resumed. A small victory in his battle with his higher self and learning his new craft. Tutu had not provided him with travel instructions and so he was working things out as he went.

While he had been 'paddling his body,' so to speak, he hadn't been paying attention to his direction. He had flown onto the lava field. When he realized that, he stopped and his spirit self collapsed onto the rock. Sharp *a'a* made him jump up. *Why am I feeling this?* he wondered. *I feel like I am me. In me.* In fact, everything hurt and he was hungry. *How can that be?* He glanced around and saw he was not on the lava he had been to before. He was not near the ocean, but up much higher. Fingers of mist wafted past and he wished for his *kapa,* even if it was only in his mind. He felt cold, however, and closed his eyes and prayed for a *kapa.* Nothing. He thought he heard Tutu's voice tell him to get on with it, but he was sure she was not with him. He just knew what she would say: "Keep going."

He sent his energy out and nothing familiar responded. He was alone. At least in terms of help. He did sense a frenetic vibration from farther in the distance. He tried to travel the spirit way, but was unsuccessful. He grumbled about Tutu and her abandonment of his education. What good was it if he couldn't use it when needed?

He began to walk in the traditional way and passed an *'ae* fern struggling to grow out of the lava. *Good luck, my friend,* he thought, *we shall both need it.* The slight slope he had been laboring up leveled and he was on a mostly flat plain. Mist or smoke rose in small columns in the distance and he still heard and felt the frantic energy. He was no closer to it, however. No plants. No water. He had never seen such bleakness. Even when he had crossed other lava flows, there was life about. He had been near the sea, or trees had been visible, even though far away. But this . . . this filled him with despair.

He sat to think. The ground was warm, but not overly. Obviously, he was near Pele's home, but he had never been here. He had heard tales . . . what could he remember? He sent out his energy. He noticed the *aka* lines were not straight and true anymore. Like a fishnet that had become tangled, they made a ball of twisted energy edged with black. What was happening to the lines?

He reached out a spirit hand and touched the lines and felt pain. He was 'open' when he touched the lines; he had not learned to protect himself well, and he felt something that made him very afraid. His fingers felt physically pierced and in that moment of agony, that second before pulling back his hand, he also felt the pain of the lines themselves. The lines, he understood, were connected to people, living and dead, at the other end. He felt their pain and fear. This vast mesh that spanned the plain at the top of the mountain held people. The ones who had been taken. Their spirits were trapped here, along with, he hoped, some he could still save.

He felt something else, too. Something kept the people captive; held them prisoner. He felt a powerful *kahuna 'ana'ana* at work. A sorcerer. Not the dark magic that every *ali'i* had for the good of the people. But a blacker magic that had taken everything good and used it, consumed it, for its own benefit. It had taken all this energy, these people, and given it to a god. Together, the sorcerer and the god wanted to rule everything.

In a blink, Coconut Man understood it was bigger than anyone, even Tutu, had seen. The world. The world of the islands; the world beyond the islands. This god and his dark priest wanted it all.

Shaken, he breathed to calm himself. Reached out an energy line to Tutu, but got no response. A tingling of another energy. Not the darkness that had frightened him, but another *kahuna.* Perhaps a priest who had been taken from the village? He was afraid and pulled back to think. How to protect himself? What had Tutu told him so long ago? *Grounding.* To ground himself. Well, he was sitting on the ground. There was more. The earth. To connect himself to the earth. Tutu had said Pele needed help. As much as one could trust a volatile goddess like Pele, he was in her lands now. He reached out to Pele.

'O Pele ko'u akua
He ali'i no la'a uli
No la'a kea
Pele is my goddess,
A chiefess of sacred darkness
And of sacred light
'O Pele ko'u akua
'O Pele ko'u akua
Kokua
Kokua
Pele is my goddess
Pele is my goddess
Help
Help

Coconut Man felt melded to the lava. His bones, his body, combined with Pele's land and he pushed out to her. His heartbeat quickened and he felt a dangerous, but decidedly female energy, respond. It was muted and he couldn't tell why. Restrained somehow. An image filled his mind. A *mamo* bird in a twig cage, like the bird catchers made. Sticky sap on a branch to hold fast the feet, so its captors could snatch it off and imprison it. Usually to pluck it raw and bare; use its feathers to make a cape for *ali'i. How interesting,* he thought. *Mamo, black feathers for ali'i's cape, and Pele, her black lava cape streaming like dried tears to the sea.*

Pele was imprisoned somewhere. Somehow. *How does one imprison a goddess?* Coconut Man could not begin to guess, except that very strong sorcery was involved. Sorcery he was ill-equipped to fight. *Except with a basket!* According to Tutu. *I am going to die.*

None the wiser, Coconut Man slowly brought his thoughts to the surface of his spirit body and stood. How many layers was that, now? His true form lay in a hollow of boulders in a valley far away. This spirit body managed to come and go with some other force of bodily might, and it, in turn, had taken another journey in *pule*—prayer to Pele.

Although he had not touched Pele directly, Coconut Man knew he had reached her. And she was aware of him. That understanding filled him with fear. Fear and pride. If he was to die, he would do it fighting for people who could no longer fight for themselves. He set off toward the columns of smoke once again, determined to free as many spirits as possible. A small thought tickled his brain: *if you die here, though you might be brave and fight valiantly, no one will ever know.*

Chapter Seven

Gray clamped down on the land as Coconut Man neared the rising smoke of the lava plain atop the mountain. A heavy lid pressed down, bringing heat and sweat, both to him and to the lava that pulsed and glowed, bled and heaved. His feet grew warm, but he continued.

He was so tired, that when he finally saw Pele's home, he just stopped. Not even surprised. A vast chasm lay at his feet. An ocean of lava, orange and red, bubbled far below. He was dizzy from the heat, the smell, the expanse, and so he sat, feeling the burn under his *malo*, but too tired to do anything but shift his weight back and forth.

When had he eaten? Or drank? Was this his spirit body or some other body? A spirit body wouldn't need to eat or drink, would it? That made no sense. His thoughts meandered and tumbled and finally stilled. This was getting him nowhere. He gathered enough strength to stand and fleetingly thought, *that is going to hurt,* thinking of his burned thighs and *'okole.*

He knew Pele was trapped inside her crater home. *How* did not matter, but he felt her there, and he sensed she felt him along the rim. He turned and headed toward the far side where he knew the dark sorcerer kept his captured spirits. A layer had been stripped off Coconut Man, and he was only sensation now; only energy, being guided by other energy. He tried to shield himself from discovery by the sorcerer but knew he was too tired to be completely successful. His hope was that he or she was too busy with dark magic to sense his approach. Pele was doing her best to distract the other god or goddess, and that was also engrossing the *kahuna 'ana'ana.*

Coconut Man had seen across the vast crater to the other side of the plain. Although it appeared flat, it was really pocked with many slight valleys and caves, lava tubes and brilliant, boiling pools. The heat was unbearable, and in the way of spirit things he had not yet figured out, sometimes he felt the heat and he was very corporeal, and other times, he was not—he simply swayed and bobbed above it all. However, no matter his own form, he felt the spirits he wanted to save, and he felt Pele, always near, fighting beside him.

Beneath all of that, was the rivalry of the other god and the anger of his dark sorcerer, pulling against Pele; wanting her, her people, and her lands. Coconut Man felt, now that he was closer in fact, on top or under, he could not tell, that Pele was fighting for her people. She thought of the village as hers and would protect it. She had been tricked into relinquishing enough of her power and she was weakened.

Without speaking, Coconut Man knew she thought of him as hers, too. He would honor her in this quest.

Cautiously, he circled the vast pit, and as he reached the other side, he heard chanting. The lava boiled up in a geyser and fell back. The chanting grew louder. As he drew nearer, the reek of metallic earth burned his eyes and the noise of the red rock fountain deafened him. He felt as much as heard the chanting of the dark priest. He could not see anyone yet. His footing slipped on ʻaʻa pebbles, cutting his leathery feet. If he had not slid in a well of his own blood and fallen, he would have missed the slit in the earth, the cave where as soon as he focused on it, he knew was the prison of the souls taken from the village.

He slithered carefully into the entrance and listened. The pulsing lava was dampered here, but the heat increased. The chanting was muted. A rustling of *kapa*, feet, breathing and the tang of fear overlaid the beat of the volcano's heart.

Pele's heart.

The entrance sloped quickly down to a larger room and fingers of flowing lava acted as light sources and to keep the villagers from exploring. He wondered why no one guarded the opening. He knew people had been taken, but he was surprised at how many there were.

Some of the younger men, the warriors, were still there, but perhaps not as many as a village might need. Strong, vibrant sacrifices would be made first, he surmised. His spirit body floated about, checking on their health. They seemed well enough, but groggy, sleepy, as if perhaps given too much *awa* to drink. When he concentrated, he smelled the rankness of the closed room and the acrid odor of Pele's home. He knew that those fumes could make one sick; when crossing

Pele's lands, one tried to avoid the huge yellow clouds that drifted across her property. In this small space, with the ribbon lava trickling past, the air was thick with poisons.

Thankfully, no *keiki.* Maybe children did not make good sacrifices to the enemy of Pele? He did not know. Perhaps, once the village had been cleansed and claimed, the *kamali'i* would be used to start a new population. The possibilities were too awful to think about. For now, he was grateful.

He saw no sign of the *kahuna 'ana'ana* in here. No chanting or magic where the captives lay. What next? The people were safe enough for now. He looked for a hole he could enlarge while he waited for a sign or instruction. Perhaps more air would help. He saw a crack and crawled over. As he examined it, he lay next to a familiar form. Very familiar. He sat up quickly and the other figure did, too. He faced himself. The other man hit his head on the low ceiling, but groggily peered about, as if unsure where he was.

Coconut Man's heart pounded and his breath came in gasps. What was this sorcery? What had happened to him? Obviously, he was no longer in the valley far away, sound asleep, waiting for help.

The real figure of himself was completely unaware of his spirit self. Coconut Man was terrified. His spirit and body had split completely, just like the others in the village. That could only mean he had been captured for sacrifice as well. The only difference was he knew he was the plaything of the gods. How that helped, he did not know, because he had no idea what came next.

He was afraid to return his spirit body to his real body. Would his knowledge evaporate like morning mist and would he be as helpless as the rest? His figure looked as though it did not know what had befallen it; how it had come here. Without seeing his mind from the inside, he did not know of his awareness. Did it remember what its task was? Perhaps he held that knowledge with this self, and upon reuniting with the physical form, the minds would meld as well.

He had to do something. That husk that lay like a lump of poi would be no help without a mind, an awareness to guide it and the others. An increase in a humming in the earth; a pressure, a rumble. Coconut Man had to make a decision. He had to help Pele, and the people had to help him. They would all have to fight together.

He saw no other way but to return his spirit self to its home. He focused all his energy, used all the techniques Tutu had shown him, called down all his ancestors, known and unknown, asked for Pele and the villagers and pressed into his own body. At the moment of moving into his own form, he saw all the spirits of the villagers in the cave with him. Shadowy forms, weakened but alive, and waiting for his guidance. He also saw Pele. Pele in all her greatness, in the walls of the cave, her arms stretched, both protecting and pleading. She was very thin, pulled taut inside the cave, and pressed through the walls of the mountain as well. Her figure ebbed and flowed and she fought an unseen opponent. She was holding on, waiting for him; waiting for him to gather his strength and that of the others and come to her aid.

When he snapped into his own body, he was disoriented. *Am I in a cave? Where is it? Who is with me?* He had fallen back against the wall and the sharp stones and heat helped bring him to consciousness.

He was in pain; his journey from the valley rock tumble to the fire cave must not have been an easy one. Bruises and cuts patterned his body like designs on *kapa.* He recognized no one among the people. Why would he? They were not his village. He peered through the gloom at the frightened and beaten faces. Even the warriors had lost hope and strength in the days of captivity.

He pushed his fear away and let his spirit knowledge through. Like a companion, it told him of its own journey and discovery. Soon he understood what had passed. Then Coconut Man pulled his energy back. He gathered it from where it had scattered these past days. He scratched it from the rocks, the dark, the bits that Pele herself had flung off in fighting her foe. As he pulled this cloak of power to him, he pressed it onto the spirits of the people in the cave. Their fear lessened and his spirit–self spoke to theirs.

Their bodies were weak, but their love for their village and their goddess was not. They were reassured when Coconut Man told them Pele was still their protector, not their adversary and attacker.

"Why is there no guard on this cave?" he asked.

"Sorcery guards it and only the dark one can enter when he brings a sacrifice," a man answered.

"Or takes one out," another whispered.

"How many have you lost?"

"More, now." A mumbling as heads were counted.

"Three that we are sure of, but we think more because Nāwai has not been seen since he went to scout for a pig on the mountain." A man stepped forward. "We were pig-hunting and saw another hunting party far away on the mountain. Nāwai went to meet them and scout the area, but we never saw him again."

"Do you think they took him?" a woman asked.

"Let me see." Coconut Man closed his eyes. His spirit body called to Nāwai. Nāwai had been staying close to his people and came forward immediately.

Coconut Man saw from his spirit form that he was dead and that made him sad. One he could not save. But perhaps, Nāwai could help them.

Aloha, he told Nāwai.

Aloha. I have been waiting for you.

For me?

Yes. You were at my death, and your energy helped me. So, this had been the man who was murdered that first night.

Helped you? How?

I was afraid. Not to die, I am a hunter, a warrior, but what I saw. . . I knew my people were in terrible trouble but then I felt you there. You are the one. Tell me how to help.

Why did they kill you? And not all these others? Where did, uh, they put you? Coconut Man didn't want to offend, but why kill him and then drag him all the way up to the top, to here?

I was a sacrifice. I was needed then, and close to that place. A boundary marker for the kahuna 'ana'ana. *A blood sacrifice. I am still there. On the lower flow. My bones are under a marker. Others mark that dark place as well.*

Where? Can we get you back?

I don't think so. But you can turn my sacrifice into protection. Pele saw.

90

Pele was angered by my death. She is covering my resting place with lava and you will turn the curse into a blessing. I am sure of this.

Mahalo, he told Nāwai. *These things I will do.*

Coconut Man shifted his body and came back to himself. When he opened his eyes, he had the disconcerting feeling of twice as many eyes on him. His grounding had strengthened his power to see, and not only did he see all the villagers, but also their spirit bodies hovering nearby. Two of everyone. He repressed a shudder.

I wonder if I will ever get used to this? he thought. He also could still see Nāwai, as well as several other wispy shapes, he imagined were lost spirits. They smiled and moved to be near him. *I suppose it would be lonely if no one could see you, or spoke or prayed to you anymore.* In fact, the cave felt very crowded now.

"I am sorry to tell you, Nāwai is dead." He paused for everyone to hear. "He is with us now, though, and wishes to help. In fact, many spirits are."

The crowd cheered up quite a bit at that and clamored for more information. "I don't have time to find out their names so we can have a lu'au now, but we will do that later."

Perhaps he should not be so irritable. This was hard for all of them. He did not repeat all the news from Nāwai. Some things he did not want to share.

"We need to pray, *pule,* for our future. Pele is helping us, herself too, but she grows tired. She needs us. I will send my spirit body out to find her and this black sorcerer. I will need all the chanting to strengthen me, to tie me to you. Whatever happens, you must not stop chanting."

In the glow of the distant lava streams, they formed two ragged circles. The people made one and the spirits another. They clasped hands and one of the older men began the *mele*. A chant for strength, a chant for unity, a chant for Pele. A prayer to bind them all until the end.

Chapter Eight

For a moment, Coconut Man allowed the power of the *pule* to lift him. He let it fill him and although he had experienced many things because of Tutu and her powers, her gifts, her expertise, he had never known this. He felt inflated, like the puffer fish, and his spirit easily lifted from its host.   This time, though, his body remained aware. Part of him was excited at this new skill. That could be helpful to see what was happening inside the cave while he was not there.   Wherever he might be.

Trepidation stilled his flight. He had not seen the sorcerer. He had not seen

Pele except in spirit form when she came to them in the cave. Was she inside the earth? More than anything in his life, he did not want to go into the bubbling crater. Even if his spirit would not burn, he could not imagine keeping his wits about him in a fuming pot of lava. The sorcerer must have a way to combat her without dying himself. In fact, his powers were so great that he had enlisted another god or goddess to help him.

Now Coconut Man was truly terrified. He began to tremble and those clasping his hands on either side must have felt it for they gripped him tighter. He slowed his breathing. He felt the calloused hand of a hunter or carver on one side, and on the other, the softer hand of an old woman he suspected was a *kahuna* of some sort. He had not learned her area of expertise, as all *kahuna* specialized in something, but the calmness she instilled in him just by her hand, said perhaps she was a healer. In fact, she reminded him of Tutu a little. But not as scary.

Grounded once more, he sent his own *aka* lines around the circle and crisscrossed it, like a spider web to a shrub, anchoring himself in this time and place. Now that he knew his physical body could slip, or be moved while his spirit was absent, he wanted to make that as difficult as possible. Each person in the circle would be bound to him, and to each other. The spirits of the villagers instinctively knew to hold on and to build each layer of chant and prayer higher and stronger, like the stone walls they made in the *ahupua'a.*

He felt ready to leave. The villagers had said the entrance was guarded. How? He floated to the opening and saw no one. No guards, spirit or human, hovered near. Perhaps only humans were guarded, and the *kahuna* was unaware some people could spirit walk?

Cautiously he moved up the slight slope to the crest of the hill. The chanting was loud and clear now, ringing off the rocks, its pull like a fishing line. It drew him to the bubbling pot of Pele's house. He still didn't see the sorcerer. The *mele* came from all directions, suffocating him and pulling him at the same time. He walked to the edge of the cliff. His spirit self felt the heat; it was stronger here, and he thought his skin would peel.

He turned away, to go back to the cave to try another approach. His path was blocked. There were guards after all. The short way from the cave slit to the precipice was lined with Night Marchers— ghosts, skeletons, spirits of warriors long dead who were doomed to walk the night on the paths they trod to their destruction. He knew the battlefields where they haunted, but how did they get here? The sorcerer must have called them to him as he did all of them; as he did Pele and perhaps even the one who fought against Pele.

This witch, this dark magician, was more powerful than he imagined. To be able to call gods and goddesses, ghosts and *kāhuna*, at his will would mean the oldest magic; from back in the old lands, *Kahiki,* perhaps. Pele and her brothers and sisters came from there. Coconut Man, his people, *all* the people came from there. This was older and darker than the stories. The only person he could have asked for help, Tutu, was not able to assist.

The Night Marchers did not speak but pressed him backward toward the edge. The stories said if you ever came upon them in your travels, not to look at them and you might be spared. It was far too late for that. For ghosts, they looked real enough. They made no sound, not a word, a breath, a footfall. Beyond him, the chanting continued and he knew he would get a close look at his adversary, however fleeting, as soon as he was pushed off the cliff.

He dropped to his hands and knees and scrabbled for a handhold; found instead whorled lava, crumbles of *a'a*, nothing to grab. The Night Marchers simply pushed. He grabbed them; they felt real, too. The whole group just walked off the cliff with him in their midst.

Before he had time to think, he hit a ledge. A wide platform, not visible from the cliff top, it ran many tree lengths along the crater, part-way down. Spirit warriors tumbled past him into the lava, eerily silent. Those who also hit the ledge picked themselves up and stood at the ready. The noises of the lava were quieter here; a strange effect of the setback, the ledge tucked into the cliffside.

The chanting, the cursing, was louder as the sorcerer neared some key point. Far down the platform, Coconut Man got his first glimpse of the *kahuna*. Layers upon layers of *kapa*, *ki* leaves, feathers, bones, and a gourd mask, costumed the whirling priest. He whipped himself to frenzy as he performed his rite, creating more danger for his victim, who now, Coconut Man saw, was a beautiful young girl at the far side of the ledge. She wore red *kapa* and stood frozen, her long hair covering her face. She seemed unable to move, except for feeble struggles, held by invisible thread.

Coconut Man knew it was Pele, in one of her weaker forms, and that her restraints were the sorcerer's own *aka* threads, woven with her in mind. How many years of plotting had this plan been in the making? Centuries? Coconut Man still did not know the author of the curse. The truth he had discovered was so much worse than he'd imagined. It was like thinking one had caught a tuna but ending up with a Tiger shark.

Coconut Man tore his eyes away from the sight and looked over the crater. Another battle raged directly over the lava; a terrible war. Pele's other self battled not one but two goddesses and the spirit of the sorcerer. Three giant powers against one. How had Pele managed to last so long?

I waited for you, he heard in his mind. *I waited for my people. I knew you would come. I grow tired and need you now.*

Even as the words were spoken calmly, the spirits fought over the inferno. Shadow forms raced and wrestled in the poisoned fog that ebbed and flowed, colors ever changing. The Night Marchers closed in on him.

Coconut Man waited no longer. He sat along the back wall of the ledge as far from the broiling heat as possible and anchored himself to the lava with his own *aka* threads. He pressed his back against the warm rock and allowed his spirit flesh to meld into it. He sank into the stone and joined the mass chant that had never stopped from those moments in the cave. The people held true. Immediately he felt Pele grab onto him, and therefore all of them, and grow in strength. He was so embedded in her lava that her pull did not loosen his grasp. His words rose, strong in the cloudy air, and the Night Marchers lost their footing and stumbled to a halt.

Without opening his eyes, he saw the mid-air battle above the crater. The two goddesses with Pele looked similar, but he did not know them. Sisters perhaps. They raged and screamed and tore at Pele, but through it all, Pele held firm, while batting away the spirit of the sorcerer. The sorcerer chanted on, but now the young girl had changed into a white-haired old woman, the *aka* threads dissolved, and she began to advance on him.

She spoke. "You do not have the power to harm me any longer. My people have come for me. I knew they would. Look! Look and see what love I have!"

Coconut Man turned and saw a chain of spirit people stretching from where he sat on the ledge to inside the mountain. He knew it led to the souls in the cave, clasping hands and chanting. The people melded to the mountain the way he melded to the ledge; their grasp was firm and unyielding. He turned back and his spirit body had moved, or had been moved, right next to Pele. He could touch her. Unfortunately, it also put him right next to the sorcerer whose arms were wet with sweat. As he shouted his curse and spun, flecks of spit flew like windblown rain. Pele managed to fight the three in the crater at the same time she spoke to the sorcerer. *And to me,* Coconut Man thought. *She is consoling me. Perhaps I will not die today.*

Pele reached down and nodded and he tentatively took her hand. It felt strangely normal, like an old woman's hand. Like the hand of the woman he sat next to in the cave. *No! That cannot be.* But the hands felt the same. The same healing, strengthening force. Now the hand pulsed with energy and light and he had to concentrate.

Pele stilled her lava pool and the level dropped lower in the crater. The *kahuna 'ana'ana* amplified further and the screams of all three goddess beings in the battle became clearer.

"This is your last fight, Pele. Give up!" shouted a glowing blue goddess.

"Kapo! I can't believe you took her side! Why would you?" Pele called.

"Namaka said she would help me. You have always been favored and I am always second, or third!" Kapo said.

"Namaka and I have not always gotten along; she is forever putting out my fires with her oceans. But here, she is far from the sea! What are you thinking Namaka?" Pele taunted.

Coconut Man now understood the three goddesses were all sisters, and to him, they sounded very much like any other fighting siblings, however more violent and powerful they were. It was true, the ocean goddess and Pele had a long-standing feud which resulted in Pele moving islands to find a home without her flames being drenched. But Kapo? Kapo had even helped Pele evade an overenthusiastic suitor, and so, weren't they friends and sisters? Kapo was also the goddess of sorcery, among other things, so perhaps it was logical that the witch court her as well. He could prey upon Namaka's eternal fight with Pele, but he had to offer something else to woo Kapo.

"Kapo. I love you, sister. We have had many good times. What has she promised you?" Pele called.

"She said—she promised me freedom and a place at her side in her kingdom."

"What kingdom?"

While this somewhat civil conversation continued, gouts of lava spewed, boulders the size of a *hale* were tossed about, and sheets of mist from deep inside the mountain spurted, only to be quenched immediately by the flames. The sister-war continued as the goddesses fought and scratched each other and the sorcerer chanted on, ever weaker against old-woman Pele and the power of the entire village.

"Oh, I see. My village. My people," Pele added. "Do you see them all here?

Do you think they will go willingly to their deaths for you? They have come for me!"

At this last, lava erupted out of the caldera and in a towering cascade, spilled over the top and rushed down the mountain. *Fortunately,* Coconut Man thought, *it ran down the other side, away from him and away from where the helpless villagers sat chanting and praying, trapped inside a slit cave.*

The goddesses screamed and followed the lava out of the crater and toward the flow and disappeared, still bickering and whirling.

The sorcerer grew weaker and dropped to his knees. Coconut Man thought it was over and tried to pull his hand from old woman-Pele's. She did not let go. Her hand grew hot as her anger mounted and she stood over the sorcerer.

"I have heard your chants. Your prayers. You thought you were so sly to keep it from me. This is my land, I know what happens here. I allow much to happen here. I am too busy to monitor every little thing you *people* do in your own scrubby world. I did make a mistake in underestimating your ability to gain allies. Namaka was no surprise, but I can best her. I have for years. But I did not suspect Kapo. I am disappointed in that."

She pushed off the mask with her foot and revealed a face familiar to Coconut Man: Moho, the headman he'd thought was weak. The one he'd thought did not even want to be headman because he had been so bad at it. So uncommanding. *Well, I underestimated something too*, he thought. Pele heard his thoughts and eyed him.

"Yes, we are alike, Coconut Man." Her face was stone, but there was kindness in her words.

"No, I mean. . . I'm sorry, goddess." He bowed his head.

"You can still be of use to me. We are not finished yet. You must turn this curse back to him."

"How do I turn that? I am not a *kahuna!*"

"You are now. I am no longer trapped and must go." She rose into the air and dissolved as screams from the continuing goddess battle reached his ears.

The sorcerer stirred on the ledge and the Night Marchers shifted their feet. He could not risk them waking up, or coming back to life, too. There was a way to turn a curse back to the sender. How? He had no time to climb out of the pit and get back to the cave and ask the people. But, he was still connected to them, through all of this; he was bound to them with *aka* threads and *pule*.

Moho began to mumble and although he was injured and reduced by Pele's attacks, he was far from finished. Coconut Man had to beat him in a chant. He had almost no experience with this and none against a powerful sorcerer. But he did have the power of Pele's people. That would have to do.

Coconut Man again anchored himself, this time more firmly. He sank into the stone and sent a wave of power along his *aka* to the people. He asked for help and guidance. Immediately a flow of instructions pulsed into his brain and before he could process the individual thoughts, each piece of information presented itself for him to use.

Get the bait. Bait, something belonging to the person to be cursed. Coconut Man pulled the mask to him. The mask was perfect because it also held Moho's sweat and hair. Powerful magic. The Night Marchers stilled with his first words after he held the mask. Moho struggled to reach him, but as Coconut Man began his reversal chant, he grew limp.

This is a death I inflict
For a life, a death
A great ka'upu bird is calling
Sounding nearby, calling out
What is the food it calls for?
A man is the food it calls for.
Thunder cracks in the heavens,

The earth quakes,
Your legs bend,
Your hands become paralyzed,
Your back hunches,
Your neck twists,
Your head breaks open,
Your liver rots,
Your intestines fall to pieces.

Coconut Man repeated this over and over again with variations on how Moho would be consumed and by what creatures. Each verse sent Moho's original curse back into him; the people he sacrificed, the lives he stole for his own use, all those spirits gathered around. Coconut Man felt the anger of the people reach a fever pitch and so he closed the prayer:

Numbness, numbness, numbness, numbness,
Spreads, spreads, spreads, spreads,
Stiffens, stiffens, stiffens, stiffens;
Your head droops, droops, droops,

Bends over, bends over,
It droops, droops
His eyes droop,
His nose droops,
His mouth droops,
His neck droops. . .

When he saw no more movement from Moho, he took the bait, the mask, and threw it into the bubbling lava. He finished with the *pule* for burning of the bait.

As he did so, he felt the sorcerer's companions—other devils so far unseen—rise to battle against him, but he was safe in the arms and *aka* of the people. The power of the group magic, the pooling of the *mana, kakulu kumuhana,* had won the day. The spirits of the people released him and before he could blink, had picked Moho up and thrown him into the crater. As his body flew over the edge and his devil companions disappeared, a shadow mingled with Coconut Man's spirit feet.

When Coconut Man awoke from his trance-state, night had fallen. In fact, he had no idea what day it was, or even how many had passed. He was alone on the ledge. No Night Marchers, no young woman or old lady met him. He remembered some things, but could not tell what was real. His spirit body felt quite real and in a great deal of pain. He looked up at the rim of the crater. A long way to go from the ledge to the top. Unsure whether his spirit form would make it or not, he called once more upon the people to help him.

Faces peered down and a young man called to him, "Coconut Man! Let your spirit rise up!" He laughed as he said this and so Coconut Man, feeling free and joyful, released his spirit and found himself at the top of the cliff.

"Go to your body now, *kahuna*," the man said. "We have much to discuss, but you have been apart from your higher and lower selves for long enough and you must be weary."

That was so. Coconut Man simply put himself back into his body. He felt at least two spirit-selves join there. He really was understanding how all this worked!

The smell in the cave was enough to make him run for the opening. The people had stayed with him until they were sure he was safe and successful in reversing the curse, so many bodies had remained in the enclosed space. While he was grateful, he could not stop his eyes from watering.

He was starving. And thirsty. Now that both spirit bodies were back with him, all his human urges rushed back full force. *All his urges.* He hobbled around to a more private spot to relief himself. He didn't know how he possibly had anything *to* relieve, but there it was.

The people milled about, finally aware. Many had been captured in the dead of night, either knocked unconscious or drugged, with no idea where they were. Moho had not bothered to feed them, so only a little food that they already had with them had been consumed, and long ago.

Their bodies were weak but their spirits strong as they recapped their victory. They thanked their ancestors for their help and celebrated their joy at seeing them again.

Coconut Man clapped his hands. "I am sorry to cut this short, but we need to go. La will come soon, and we need to be off the mountain. There is no food or drink here, but I think I can guide us to the forest at least, for water and fruit." He wondered if the older folks, the *kupuna*, could make it that far. They would just have to carry those who were unable. Once again, their group power, *mana*, would have to be enough.

Coconut Man approached the man who had first called to him from the crater rim. He seemed a capable fellow and in good health. Depressingly young and vibrant after the ordeal. Coconut Man sighed. "Will you help me organize them? I know the way out, but many are weak and may need help. What is your name? I am sorry. I am Coconut Man."

"I know who you are. It will be my honor to assist one so great and powerful. I am Kaiki."

Coconut Man preened a little at the flattery. Kaiki. That was a familiar name. Obviously a warrior. Pua! The *wahine* from the village who agreed to help him. Her husband. He was relieved to find Kaiki alive and so well.

Coconut Man checked each person and found no serious injuries, but as he suspected, many were weak. He found 'Oloa, the man who had been taken the night he found the village. He was among the oldest and weakest, but cheerful at his rescue. The older woman who had clasped his hand on the other side was in good health too, so he asked her also to help him keep track of the people. He found out her name was Ana and placed her in the middle of the group. Something in her eyes said he was right, that she was a *kahuna*, and when he saw her do her own checks of the people, holding their hands and asking questions, he was sure she was a healer. Perhaps with other skills as well.

Again, he was grateful no children had been taken.

As La's chariot rose in the east, the raggedy band began its journey homeward. Because of the health of most of them, he headed downhill and across the flow, away from the burning mouth but toward the sea. A small doubt rose up in him. Although it was in the general direction of the village, it was also the way the three screaming goddesses had gone. He knew enough about Pele and her sisters now to be sure, they had not made peace. In fact, he was sure that just because he could not hear them, did not mean that some sort of spiritual stampede was brewing.

He kept those thoughts to himself and focused on getting his people to water, food, and a safe place to rest.

Chapter Nine

The initial momentum of freedom and safety carried them for a couple hours, but the forest was still out of view when the oldest members of the group began to flag. Without sources of water and food, the weakest could not continue. Coconut Man called a halt.

"Kaiki and Ana, please come to me," he called. Upon joining him they all sat on the warm lava. Coconut Man's ankles were quite sore from traversing the uneven ground. He thought he had twisted one in the earlier race to the sorcerer and the ensuing battle. Although they had walked slowly this morning, the rolling of pebbles underfoot made travel hazardous, especially to those with old bones and not enough food.

"I think we will have to carry at least some of the *kupuna*. They will not make it to the forest. Who have you noticed is in need?"

They rested and figured out which of the youngest and strongest could help with the weakest. Kaiki offered to run and see how far the forest was, but Coconut Man was reluctant to let one of the most resilient go ahead. He was not entirely sure the trip would be safe for a single man, however warrior-like.

"If we had gone up the mountain, I could have gauged how far the forest is more accurately, and I think we would have reached it by now. However, that was a much harder path. Although it is farther and at an angle this way I think down was the better choice. As Pele spreads her lava to make more land in victory over Namaka, we may reach the trees when La is nearly finished for the day."

Kaiki nodded. Ana shrugged. "I defer to you, Coconut Man," she said. "I have not been here before. My *kahuna* family has spoken of this, but I have not seen this land, except in vision walks." She looked around at the bleak, rippled landscape. "It is daunting."

"It is that," Kaiki agreed. "Shall we pair up and gather our packages?" His eyes twinkled with good spirit.

Coconut Man smiled and eased himself creakily to his feet. Indeed, his ankles, in fact, his legs entirely, were throbbing. Ana was watching and made a 'stop' gesture. He stilled. She took both her hands and clasped his upper thigh tightly and held it. Then she muttered a few words and pulled down tightly, tugging the hairs in an unpleasant manner. She repeated it several times until he felt he could not have his leg hairs ripped anymore. As she moved to the other leg and he was about to beg her to stop, he realized the first leg had stopped aching completely. The bones felt strong and straight, the muscles no longer burned and torn. He gladly let her rip out the other leg's hairs and in a few moments, that limb was healed.

"Mahalo!" he hugged her, however inappropriate an action that was. "Can you do something with the old people, too? Heal them so they can travel more easily?"

"I have already done what I can. The lack of food has made their own healing more difficult, and of course, their age. I cannot reverse aging. You, you are different."

"I keep hearing that, but I don't know how."

"I don't either. That is beyond the scope of my learning. I only know it is so."

"We need to get going," Kaiki said. "Your magic isn't going to last forever and I am anxious to see Pua and my Precious One as soon as I can."

"Yes, let's get your packages and go," Coconut Man said with a smile. Kaiki laughed and trotted back to collect his old people and shore up the flagging spirits of his charges.

Ana headed back to the middle of the group and did the same. Coconut Man felt much better, not only in his balding legs, but much cheered in manner.

The group made it almost a whole hour before the earth split in front of them and a wave of lava flooded their path. A geyser of seawater spewed next, the water boiling in its fury to race with the lava.

Coconut Man jumped back, narrowly missing a fall into the crack in the earth. He reversed all of Ana's healing in an instant, but avoided a painful injury or perhaps even death. The land trembled as slabs of cooling lava competed with the newly freed river of orange fire. Namaka had found a way to send her ocean up through tunnels in the rock and shower them all with fountains of sea water. Kapo swirled nearby, wringing her hands but unable to intervene between her two more powerful sisters.

Coconut Man was able to see all three goddesses but wasn't sure if the others could as well. Perhaps they saw only the lava and crashing waves. Was Kapo manifested as the wind? He didn't know since he saw them all. He pressed back and guided his people farther from the battle zone. On a slight rise, he saw they were near the coast where Pele's dripping flames made more land and Namaka's waves endeavored to extinguish them.

To the group's left, he saw the tops of palms and his heart lifted. Between the people and the forest was a huge mound of cooled lava. They would have to go back up a considerable distance or navigate closer to the edge of the sea to avoid the obstacle. Pele and Namaka screamed and fought; Namaka snatched chunks of Pele's hair and threw them aloft for Kapo to bat about while Pele plunged her fiery fingers deep into the seabed, attempting to dislodge Namaka's hold on the beach.

Coconut Man felt strange. He wanted to be near the battle. He led the group down toward the ocean and the great rift in the earth. The closer he got, the more he wanted to be in the thick of it. His charges trailed reluctantly until they were all on a cliff above the ocean. The lava spilled into the sea from a tube inside the mountain; gouts of yellow steam billowed, making visibility difficult. Through his visions, Coconut Man knew exactly where he was. He began to chant, to urge Namaka and Kapo to victory.

"Coconut Man!" Kaiki shouted. "What are you doing? That is dangerous!"

Coconut Man heard, but paid no heed. The words did not make sense. He whipped up the battle, calling and taunting Pele to give in. His eyes glazed, unseeing as he edged toward the precipice. Kapo's winds pushed him and Namaka's sizzling steam enveloped them all.

He tripped, falling in a heap, his ankles weak once more. His people clustered together, muttering and terrified.

Ana called to Kaiki, "He is possessed! He now sides with Kapo and Namaka against Pele. This cannot stand. We must *pule*!"

Some of the oldest had collapsed on the hot rock and lay, too weak to move. She gathered them as best she could. They all grasped hands and began a chant.

Coconut Man observed all of this, but it had no impact. He was strong inside; power grew in him like rising tide, filling him. Pele was not his goddess, not his protector. He had made a bargain with Namaka and Kapo for power. He would control this village, this island! These goddesses needed him. They desired to control Pele and her lands as he desired to control these weak minds to his own ends. His dark magic grew as Pele's power weakened.

He had been smart to lie in wait for this kahuna, *this Coconut Man who did not know his own potential. How does someone not know what lies within himself? What dreams lie dormant until bursting forth in a rush of power? He would control this human plane soon enough. This paltry whining he heard from the old ones on the lava. The weak ones. He had done well to bring them here many days ago, keeping them for this moment when he would sacrifice them to Namaka and Kapo.*

The small part of Coconut Man who was still truly him heard this in his own head and his bowels turned to water. He knew what had happened and that nothing was over; the people were not safe. Moho had not been vanquished on the ledge. His essence had crept inside Coconut Man and hidden at the last moment. Stayed well below the surface until he had guided his pawn to this place of danger where liquid land met sea and gale-force winds threatened to toss them all into the ocean to boil.

Namaka and Kapo did their parts. The long shelf where all the people lay gasping and chanting was weak. The lava tubes, the crushing wind sucked the support out from under the rock. Dense, toxic, yellow clouds covered the area. Easy to make a false turn.

Coconut Man-Moho had plotted well with his conspirators. Pele could not fight them all, and now that Coconut Man sided with Moho, all seemed lost.

Moho's eyes glittered as he joined in with his own dark curse. He pulled his battered host's body up to standing and turned to face the group, filthy and exhausted, but undaunted as they lay, hands clasped, praying and fighting him to the last.

The goddess' fight reached a crescendo of water, steam, lava, wind and noise as the chanting rose to meet it. The rock could take no more. The shelf cracked. A huge section of land, as big as the center of their village, began to give way. The people felt it first and tried to scrabble back. In their weakened condition, it was fruitless. They began to slide toward the boiling sea. Moho spun and cursed, stomped and wove his spell with his borrowed body. He grew stronger and fed off the goddess' battle. Pele, always in tune with her people, despite her claims not to care, felt them slide.

She flew to the shelf but it was too late. She could not stop it. She could not save both her people and her *kahuna,* Coconut Man, this strange human from far away, who gave all, sacrificed all, for her, and for people he had never met before a few previous journeys of La. She made a choice.

Chapter Ten

Pele reduced her lava in the tubes under the breaking shelf. She hardened a section and pushed the boiling river to another rock face. The shelf slowed its fall but did not stop it entirely.

Coconut Man-Moho was insane with power and self-importance. "You will heed me, Pele!" he cried. "You will be at my command!" He danced and writhed even as his footing gave way. "All will bow before me!" Then he made his mistake. "Even you!" He pushed his chant out to include Namaka and Kapo. "You will all be mine!"

Gods and goddesses are all powerful but they are also fickle, taking as much as they give, ignoring the lives of man when it suits them. But when attention is asked for, it is often granted, whether or not the attention is truly desired.

Namaka and Kapo stilled. The eye of the storm, the calm in the midst of fury. They faced Moho. When seconds before they had been willing to kill Pele to gain her land and worshippers, now they instantly allied with her against the human who thought himself more powerful than a goddess.

Only the smallest part of Coconut Man was still inside the husk. Moho controlled so much of him. He looked out beyond Moho's eyes and saw the terror in his people. The way they clung to each other and the tipping rock. He saw Kaiki and a few of the stronger men struggling to push the people up the ever-steepening slope onto stable land; people screaming and crying; Ana and a few still praying and chanting even as they hoisted others to safety.

Pele had done her best to move the lava but the ocean still steamed just below where the people would fall to their deaths.

He could not let Moho win. Moho might not survive the goddess' wrath, but he could still hurt or kill innocents. Coconut Man had to distract Moho and keep his curse from collapsing the ledge and gaining power from so many human sacrifices. Whatever Moho thought, Coconut Man knew Pele would not want her people to die for her this way. The tiny bit of him that still existed knew he only had moments to decide. He knew if he died, the people would be saved. He knew it. He jumped off the ledge into the burning sea.

Pele had built enough support under the collapsing shelf to stop it at last. Her people were safe for the moment. When Coconut Man–Moho jumped, Namaka and Kapo reached to embrace him. Pele understood that Coconut Man, her man, was still somewhere inside the crazed

Moho spirit. She would save him as she had others who served her in the past. The Moho spirit did not want to die but was perfectly willing to let Coconut Man sacrifice himself. The Moho spirit just needed another host and flew out of Coconut Man when he jumped. He had not counted on the rage of the goddesses. Pele and her sisters worked together as only they could when they were not feuding. Namaka and Kapo pushed a violent plume of cold water and wind up to throw Coconut Man back onto the rock ledge. The instant Moho left Coconut Man's body, Pele snatched him with a splash of lava which was joined by boiling water and swirling winds. Instantly, he was sucked under writhing waves of lava and water and disappeared. Pele made sure anything remaining that was human was destroyed. The combined strength of the sisters consumed his spirit being, the selfish kahuna willing to sacrifice all for ultimate power.

Typical of goddesses, they immediately abandoned their other humans and set off to reunite and celebrate.

Coconut Man came to on the ledge above the sea. No screaming. No fighting of goddesses or signs of spiritual battle. Only wind, waves and the spill of a relatively gentle flow of lava into the sea.

His head hurt and probing found a fist-sized lump. He felt as if he'd been beaten, which when he thought about it, he had. The last he remembered was standing on the edge of the ledge as it slithered toward the water. He remembered deciding to jump into the water to save his people, but now he lay on the warm rock, clearly not dead. Unless only spirit remained. That was possible, and somehow, was all right, too. He opened his eyes and saw the people in various positions of rest, many facing him with looks of anticipation.

As his gaze moved from face to face, he realized these were his people, too. He had grown as fond of them as those in his other village. They had risked all together, and for each other. That was something. Ana came to him and began her questions and touching–healing.

"My head hurts," he told her. She immediately placed her warm hands on the lump and gently pressed. The pain melted. He sat up. The people audibly exhaled.

"We've been waiting for you," old 'Oloa said.

"How long?" Coconut Man asked.

"There he is!" Kaiki called as he came over. "Done with your nap now?" His smile was warm and held a hint of what? Fear? Concern? Coconut Man thought Kaiki spoke for them all when he felt Kaiki's worry that he was dead, and had sacrificed himself to save the rest of them.

"Yes, I am. *Mahalo* for asking." Coconut Man rose. "If you are all rested too, perhaps we should head back?"

Despite their worry and fatigue, and even those who thought they were at the end of this life, all cheerfully struggled to their feet. They held onto each other, not because they had to in order to travel, but because they needed contact, that closeness after everything they had suffered and seen.

Kaiki placed his group at the end again, and Ana held forth in the middle. Coconut Man once again led the group, and 'Oloa came to walk with him. They could only travel as fast as the slowest member, and that was fine with Coconut Man. He felt as old as 'Oloa looked.

Since they had come downhill to the ocean they now only had to cross the flat lava away from La's path to reach the forest. After just a little walking, Coconut Man pointed to the tops of palms in the distance, indicating the forest was near. The group sighed and Coconut Man thought they would make it. He cautioned himself because the last time he thought that, a huge piece of land had fallen from under their feet and the largest war in his memory had ensued.

"What made you do it?" 'Oloa asked him, bringing him out of his reverie.

"Do what?" Coconut Man asked.

"Jump. Why did you jump into the ocean?"

Coconut Man thought back. Much of what had happened was lost to him. Moho had completely taken control of him and his own spirit had been so small that he had no memory.

"I am not sure. I remember standing on the ledge as it was falling into the water. Moho had taken me over." He glanced at 'Oloa. "Could you see that? Did you know it was not me in my skin?"

"Most of us did not know but Ana did. We knew you would not hurt us after protecting and helping us for so long, but we did not know exactly what was happening."

"I don't remember what I did after that. What did you see?"

"We saw and heard you chanting to Kapo and Namaka against Pele. We knew something was wrong, but we kept up our chant. We didn't know what else to do."

"Moho possessed me at that point. He had hidden in me and I did not know. He came out at that crucial moment to push me into hurting Pele. He was so swollen with power that he thought he controlled all the goddesses. That was his mistake."

"You could see them? The goddesses?"

"Yes. They are beautiful and terrifying. I do not need to see them again. I know I will meet Pele, but many do, so that can't be helped." Coconut Man sighed. "What did it look like?"

"Terrible winds picked up everything and flew it around our heads: pebbles, Pele's hair, leaves, seaweed, branches, seafoam. The waves got higher and higher, as with the winter storms that wipe out villages, and the lava splashed above the ledge we stood on; the river of red rushed to the sea and where they met . . ." 'Oloa trailed off, his face frozen in fearful memory. "The noise. I will never forget the noise. Among the wind, sea, and lava it was like screaming."

"It was screaming. Those goddesses never stopped screaming," Coconut Man said.

'Oloa turned a startled face to him. "You have seen much."

"Too much. And I am sure it is not the last time."

"It is not over?" 'Oloa's face paled.

"No, no. This is over. I am sure of it now. But, for me, I think I am just beginning. Tutu is quite the teacher. Not a good one, however," Coconut Man said grimly.

"Who is Tutu? Your Grandmother?"

"Not literally. She is my teacher. And a troublemaker," he added. But what if she was? In some way his grandmother? How would that work? His head began to ache.

"But why did you jump?"

"Oh, that. I would rather kill myself and take Moho with me than let him hurt our people and our goddesses. He had only dark plans and I knew I could not let that happen."

"Our people?" 'Oloa smiled.

"Yes. Well. Anyway, I realized my mistake as soon as I jumped because Moho left me. I don't know what happened after that. I thought I had died."

"After you jumped, a big wave of water pushed out of the sea and the terrible wind threw you back onto the ledge. We thought you were dead, too." 'Oloa threw his arm over Coconut Man's shoulders. "I am glad you are not."

"Yes. Me, too." Coconut Man glanced sideways at this old, old man, who was just happy to be alive, and decided he too, was happy to be alive. He adjusted 'Oloa's arm to support him better and stretched his neck from the strain of looking only at the rippled lava at their feet.

The trees were just ahead! They had reached the forest. He called to the group that they would rest in the shade, out of the beating of La's rays. Even at the end of the day, heat bounced off the black rock.

The people hobbled faster and collapsed under the cover of the moist jungle. Coconut Man even thought he knew where they were. He dragged himself to Kaiki to confirm.

"I think we are close to the village. Is that so? Have you been here hunting?"

"No, but I can check," Kaiki said. And before Coconut Man could ask what he meant, Kaiki had scurried up a tall palm. *The young. They have such energy,* Coconut Man thought dispiritedly.

Moments later Kaiki was back. "I saw the smoke from cook fires," he said. He pointed in a direction that was not where Coconut Man had thought.

"Oh, well," Coconut Man said. "That's good. Can we make it before La is completely gone?"

"I have a better idea. I will run ahead and get the people to help us. If you start toward the village and I gather the rest to meet you, we will have more strength and I will bring food and water."

"Run?" was all Coconut Man could say. He nodded his assent. Kaiki took off in an instant.

Coconut Man explained the plan to the others. Since he had not seen the smoke himself and had neglected to ask Kaiki the distance, he told them not to rush. They slowly gathered themselves and shuffled in the direction they all had seen Kaiki take. Fortunately, they did not have to rely solely on Coconut Man for direction. Once they began, others recognized where they were and in a short while, a joyous mid-jungle reunion took place.

Chapter Eleven

In the village, the group was embraced and fed. *Kapu* was set aside and all ate and celebrated together. After nearly losing the entire male and *kāhuna* population, they only wanted to be near each other.

Coconut Man watched the reuniting of couples, and families, including Pua, Kaiki, and Hiwahiwa. A twinge of, not jealousy exactly, but longing filled him and he thought of Lele and Kaleo. He must start back right away. But after his business here was finished.

Ana was indeed a healer expert, and Liloa was the *kahuna* for farming. Old

'Oloa was in charge of the fish ponds but the hunting *kahuna* as well as many others were lost. This village would need time and much healing—aloha—love to recover, even a little. The loss of so many of their people was a heavy blow. For now, the joy of the return of many would sustain them, but over time, the deep loss would be felt.

Happily for some, they knew they would see their family spirits when they *pule*—or sat *ho'oponopono*—but others would have a harder time with only ethereal assistance. After all, even though Coconut Man had seen the village's spirit-members, they could not hunt or fish or farm. That was left to the living members.

He had a question for Ana. Well, many, but he started with the one he had been mulling for some time. He sat near her as she cuddled her grandson, an infant sound asleep in her arms.

After the proper greetings, he began. "I am wondering why your, well, all of your, family spirits did not tell you, any of you, what was happening? They all rushed to me and helped, but why would they not assist you in your *pule* or at least warn you?"

"It is true," Ana said. "Our spirits are with us and often aid us in our work and prayer. When people disappeared, we asked them for guidance, but it seems that as soon as our villagers went, the spirits went, too. 'Oloa is the only one who received any kind of warning from his wife who died recently. Perhaps because it was recent? I don't know. I am not a ghost *kahuna*. I don't know such things."

"But you are a healer. Doesn't that mean you work with the spirits, too?" Coconut Man was puzzled. Tutu worked a great deal in the spirit world, and now he did, too.

"No. I only work with the healing spirits, and those do not seem to cross over into other areas. At least not for me. I am not as powerful as you, Coconut Man. You have great potential and I can tell you are only at the beginning of your journey."

"What did 'Oloa's wife say? And what happened to her ghost?"

"She only told him that death was on the way. He told us, but he is so old he thought he meant he would soon join her. We in the village did not know at that time that a pattern was emerging and that more people would be taken, or that anything this terrible would or could happen."

"I suppose people do disappear from time to time?" he asked.

"Yes. This is a dangerous world. Living near Pele's lands the way we do, sometimes people get hurt and we don't find them in time. Hunting boar is dangerous, as is fishing. Bringing forth a child is dangerous, so yes, we have much death. But usually, our family ghosts are near to us." Ana shifted the sleeping baby who smacked his lips in imagined nursing. Ana continued. "'Oloa thought his wife's ghost was afraid. That was the only other thing he mentioned. 'Oloa said it might mean he would die a painful death, but really, nothing he was concerned about.

After that, no family received a visit or answer to a prayer. All the family ghosts were too scared to come to us. So, when more people vanished, and none of the family ghosts came, we knew it was something terrible. We sent out the runner, and he never came back." Ana shifted the infant to burp it.

"Who told you I was coming? You said no family ghosts came after that. Everyone seemed to know I was coming." He tossed a stick into the blaze. "Well, not me specifically, it seems, but a stranger who would help. How did that happen?"

"It is odd. You know we are visited in dreams, or we travel in dreams?"

"Of course. You do not have to be magical or *kahuna* for that!"

Ana narrowed her eyes. "That was not meant to be answered."

"I'm sorry. Go on."

"We all had the same dream one night. No one mentioned it at first because we did not know we all had it. Once we began to discuss it, we became even more afraid. I am not sure that has ever happened before; a whole village or people dreaming the same thing."

"I have never heard of that." Coconut Man thought of Tutu. As his own village's *kahuna* with such power, could she have put this dream into these people? The dream must have happened before he even left his home village. Before he had even thought of travel. In fact, Tutu had been the one to suggest a visit would be a good thing. For his trade, she said. He sighed. Did she have that kind of power? He had no idea.

Another thought occurred to him. He knew who did have that kind of power, and who had already made herself known to him and who considered him hers. Pele. Pele could very well have put the dream into the people. But for Tutu to get him to come here, to answer the dream, that meant Pele and Tutu were connected. Now his head truly spun.

"What?" Ana asked. "You are making noise. Are you in pain?"

"Only in my head," he answered.

"Your head hurts again? That was a big lump." She made to put the baby down.

"No, no. It doesn't hurt like that. I have just thought of something. A difficult concept for me."

"Can I help?"

"Not with that. But I made a promise to Nāwai's spirit that I would change his curse to a blessing. I need your help with that. Maybe everyone's help."

"Of course. Tomorrow, we will make preparations."

"More spirits than Nāwai's walks the lava fields. We must bless them all. We cannot move or relocate their bones, Pele did her best to protect them, so we must allow their spirits to walk free."

The next day many people awoke commenting that they felt they were waking from a dream. People they loved were gone, but most of the village seemed normal.

Coconut Man and Ana made plans for the blessing and called the people to meet that night for a feast and ceremony. An imu was dug to cook the pig in the ground all day. Everyone seemed eager to help ready the village for the important prayers.

A family altar stone was selected for the evening's pule. The *Pōhaku o Kāne*, a single stone monument, was surrounded by *ki* leaves and only the men were offered the ritual food. Coconut Man was appointed to give the prayers, despite his weak protests and lack of experience. In the eyes of the village, he was the expert—the *kahuna*—now and none other would serve. Much of his day was spent in worry regarding the exact prayer and ritual, not only to appease the people but also to please the gods and achieve the goal of healing the village and releasing the spirits of Nāwai and others.

His oft-made prayers for his best weaving would not do, he felt. The prayers he made throughout the day, as did all the people, whether fishing, blessing a house, farming, any task at all, were not special enough. Yet, he did not know any 'special' prayers since he was not *kahuna*. So, all day, he prayed for guidance; prayed Pele would help him and see him through his task. All day, he had no sign from her that she heard or would help.

As evening approached, the black pig was removed from the *imu* and the men served it. People sang and chanted, danced and ate. Far too soon it was time for Coconut Man.

He took a calabash of salt water and dipped a *ki* leaf, splashing droplets around the seated villagers. This *pī kai* cleansed the people and prepared all for what was to come.

As he was about to begin his main prayer, he chanced a quick plea to Tutu for assistance. He did not understand why Pele had abandoned him after all they had been through. Tutu's face appeared and smiled, but was quickly replaced by another he did not recognize. A young, strong-looking face that also smiled and nodded. He knew at once she was a goddess, but which one?

Tutu's voice came. *"Makuāhinē."* Mother? What was she talking about?

Then the woman-goddess spoke, *"Keīkīkanē."* Son.

Tutu again. "Uli is your mother. *Pule* to her. She has been waiting for this moment."

Coconut Man staggered. The *ki* leaf faltered. The people fell silent. The *kapa* robe sagged as his arms fell, nearly dropping the calabash with sea water.

He collapsed to his knees and carefully set the bowl and leaf aside on a mat. He closed his eyes and saw the goddess Uli again, smiling and nodding. As shocking as this revelation was, it was a comfort to have at least one answer. He knew what to do, and whom to ask for help.

He took a deep breath and centered himself, pulling all his spirit guides and *hanai ohana*—adopted family—from the other village to him.

> *Kūlia e Uli, ka pule kālana ola*
> Lift up, O Uli, the purified prayer for life
> *Kūlia i ke'alohi-lani la, e kūlia!*
> Lift up to the shining heavens, lift!
> Kūlia i ke kūpua o lani nei!
> Lift it to the gods of places on high!
> *'Owai ke kūpua o luna nei?*
> Who are the gods of places on high?

Coconut Man's prayer went on, asking Uli for advice, honoring her and her own family of gods, and finally releasing the prayer to bring back information to correct the wrong.

> *E hele no a maliu mai a*
> Go thou prayer but return again to me

As the prayer was freed, Coconut Man was also free to stand once again.

> *'Eli'ele kapu, eli'eli noa*

151

The sacredness has been profound, it is
now freed
Noa ke ku, noa ka hele
Freed that I may stand, that I may walk
Noa i kānāwai a ke akua
Freed by the decree of the gods

Now that the prayer was freed, Coconut Man would have to wait to receive an answer to his request for help; some sign that the *iwi*—bones—have been blessed and the curse of the sorcerer nullified.

The torches were extinguished, the people dissipated. Coconut Man hoped to receive his answer in tonight's dream. He could not leave this village and return to his own without finishing what he had begun.

As he lay on his sleeping mat in the men's *hale*, he thought again of Uli. If Tutu was right, and he had no reason to doubt her, he was the son of a goddess. That explained her comment of him being born of no woman. Who was his father?

He would tackle that question another day. Perhaps that answered his other questions of why and how he had been chosen for Tutu's lessons, and why now?

Or perhaps not. He had no idea why what was happening to him was in fact happening. Tutu might tell him if she knew, but she often kept things to herself, waiting for him to figure it out, much to his dismay.

His eyes grew heavy. He had a mother! A goddess for a mother. It could be wonderful and terrible, as all interactions with gods could be. At least his mother was not Pele! A tickle in his mind told him Pele had heard him.

His stomach clenched and sleep was a bit longer in coming this night.

Chapter Twelve

The dream came as soon as Coconut Man was fully asleep in the men's sleeping *hale*. He and his newly discovered mother, Uli, goddess of resuscitation, health, life— well-being, were walking along the lava fields together. The rolls of solid, cooled lava all looked the same at first glance, but when Uli stopped at various places, he noticed the ground glowed. He knew at each spot dwelt the *iwi*—bones—of a sacrifice. Pele had done her best to protect that spirit with her lava, but in doing so, had trapped it there. The sorcerer's curse ensured the spirit if it could not serve him, would be unable to free itself or to help others—whether they be its own family, or other gods and goddesses. Moho had been a powerful enchanter.

In the way of dreams, they covered much ground in their spirit walk and although Coconut Man's mind spun with questions in his waking world, in this one, he was content to concentrate all his energies on freeing the spirits. Uli was a beautiful goddess and he could see how a man would be unable to resist her. What he did not know, and did not ask, was, why she had chosen a human to lie with, and specifically, his father whom he did not know.

Suddenly they were at the edge of the lava field, very much like the forest where he had led the people after their escape from the goddess battle. He knew Uli and he had completed their task of freeing and releasing the spirits from the curse. Satisfaction filled him and he turned to Uli to thank her, but instead, dread replaced his contentment when he saw Pele standing on the brink of the lava. Uli had moved back into the forest but remained and that offered him small comfort. Pele wore flaming red and a younger woman incarnation. She was not a girl, nor an old woman, but more of a mother figure. Even in his dream, this puzzled him.

He dropped to his knees. "Oh, Pele, *mahalo* for all you have done for me, and for the people of this village. They have always loved and worshipped you, but now, their hearts are filled with new fealty."

"Stand, you," she said fondly. "I see you know a little of who you are." She gestured to Uli.

"Yes. Some." He tried to focus on Pele, but her flaming figure burned his vision and he could not really tell what she looked like. Only a sense of intense eyes, and long flaming hair that spun around her head though there was no wind. Her *kapa* was aflame as well, and as it too moved in the fire-wind, he saw long, strong legs planted into the field, dropping right into the earth. He shuddered.

"Uli is my sister, too. Do you know what that means?"

He nodded. He was afraid he did. He was also related to Pele. Perhaps that was why he had power here; power to help this village that worshipped her.

"I will tell you something else, Coconut Man."

He was not sure he could take anything else. The heat Pele generated made him feel sick, but he was afraid to move away, that it would insult one of the most powerful of the goddesses in the islands. Probably the world; he did not know, but he grew dizzy. He weakly nodded his assent.

"Your Tutu," she eyed him, seeing if he paid attention. He was definitely paying attention now. "Your Tutu is also my daughter."

His mouth fell open. "Ah," he tried.

"Yes. One of many I have brought into the world. So, little human, you are also related to her. Now, does that answer your question?"

His head reeled with the information. Yes, it did answer the question of why Tutu was so interested in this village, and why she was bent on teaching him so quickly. It did not answer many others such as why she had not told him herself; why she was unable to help her own mother in this endeavor; why he had never had any powers or training, teaching of any kind, until he had reached Tutu's village.

Pele's laugh filled the mountain. "Your Tutu did not tell you because she thought you were not ready to know. I disagree."

Coconut Man felt Tutu's ire rise from this far away. Her face appeared as always, large and looming, but this time, her displeasure was toward her mother. Her mother! Pele continued to laugh.

Hanau ō ke ahī. My daughter of fire. I release you from your confinement."

Tutu made a noise only described as "Humph."

"What! What is happening?" Coconut Man shouted. "I do not understand."

"My daughter," Pele began, "disobeyed me, long ago. Her punishment was a limit of her quite substantial powers. That included coming to these lands, trying to aid me. I release her from that now. She was able to get you to assist her and me, both. Clever girl." She smiled proudly at the floating head that was her daughter.

"Mother." Tutu smiled and Coconut Man saw the young, lovely woman she must have been under her wrinkles.

"I'm so confused." Coconut Man still kneeled on the warm lava. Uli came and offered her hand to help him up.

"No matter, son. We are all here to help you now. It is time to return to your village. It needs you. A little boy wants to call you father."

Coconut Man's thoughts flew to Lele and Kaleo. "Yes, I miss Kaleo, too."

"He does, but there is a new boy waiting for you now. You need to go." Uli gave him a little nudge and he stepped off the ledge of lava onto the forest floor, meeting it with a jolt that woke him.

A bit disoriented, he woke surrounded by the men's faces staring down at him.

"Well? Have you fixed everything?" 'Oloa demanded.

"I, uh, think so." Coconut Man struggled to sit up. The circle of men backed off a little and Liloa handed him a calabash of water. He drank thirstily.

"What happens next?" 'Oloa asked.

"I think you just go back to rebuilding your village."

"You think, or you know?" Liloa asked, hands on hips. "We can't make any mistakes right now where the gods are concerned."

"The gods are fine," Coconut Man said. "They have their own problems. Just go about your business. I need to return home." He stood on shaky legs.

Home. That felt nice to say. "Anyway, the spirits are free now and will come to visit you in dreams again. Eventually," he added to cover himself in case they were busy as well. Who knew what they did when gods and spirits were not attending to the issues of man? As he had discovered, they were just as fickle and fallible as man, and just as entangled in matters of the heart.

He spent the day finishing the basket and hat orders and saying good-bye to those he had grown close to during the punishing time on the mountain. It was especially difficult to say good-bye to Kaiki, Pua and little Hiwahiwa.

The village gave him a lovely farewell feast, but really, he just wanted to go home. He slept fitfully for several hours but gave up when the moonlight glowed so brightly he knew he could walk the trail at night. Perhaps he could make the journey in one arduous day? He would try.   His longing to feel his own sand beneath his feet, to bathe in the healing waters of the Wai river, and see Lele's shy smile drove him on.   He even left his samples as gifts; partly to save himself carrying them, and partly because he wanted to leave more of himself in this place.

He filled his water calabash and gathered as much food as he could carry. He would not assume he would find food along the way this time.   The moon was still high when he set off, his heart light.

Chapter Thirteen

As Coconut Man neared his home village, he sent his thoughts to Tutu. She responded immediately and by the time he entered the village itself, many of the people had gathered to greet him. It felt a little odd since he had been no one of consequence for so long.

Io the net maker clapped him on the back. He was still damp from his day of fishing but the smell and feel of the ocean comforted Coconut Man. It was so *Io*. Behind him was his daughter, Honu, and since Honu and Kaleo were seldom separated by more than a hair's breadth, he looked for the boy.

Kaleo's yell and charge at him through the crowd should not have surprised him, but it did. As did the boy's launch into his arms. He staggered, trying not to collapse under the squirming weight of a small, excited boy. Kaleo slithered to the ground, talking non-stop, while others of the village tried to greet Coconut Man as well.

He was guided toward the eating *hale* and Coconut Man knew he would have to tell the story of his adventure. He caught Tutu's eye and she frowned, giving a brief shake of her head.

Coconut Man wondered what that meant and disengaged from the group saying, "I must pay my respects to Tutu first." She was of such status in the village that this was accepted, as no other female member might be.

They touched foreheads and inhaled each other's breath, as was the customary greeting. She feigned weakness from joy and he guided her to his seating log by the river for some privacy. He doubted anyone was fooled since they all lived with Tutu, but it was an acceptable ruse.

"I know you have just returned from a great victory," she began, "but you must not speak of anything you saw or did. Beyond basket-making," she added.

"Won't they talk? Didn't everyone hear of the troubles in that village? How am I to explain that?"

Tutu's face took on a speculative look and she gazed into the middle distance. "My daughters and I have taken care of that."

"What do you mean? Taken care of? Half a village disappears and no one is going to ask questions?"

"A fever swept through the village before you arrived. You are safe and have not brought sickness with you. A *ho'oponopono* was done and the problems that caused the illness are resolved. You had nothing to do with that."

"What did I do the whole time, then?"

"What you do best. You wove baskets and hats, fostered good will between villages. Made friends." She smirked a little at the last since they both knew he was not skilled at making friends.

"What makes you think that is the story the whole village will tell? What is in it for them?"

"Moho is dead. Truly dead, so there is no danger of him repeating his curses or hunger for power. We used our dream walking to convince the village of what happened."

Coconut Man raised his eyebrows, *yes*?

"Much like we spoke to you, only our conversation was real. Theirs was not."

"How do I know what happened in my dream was real?"

Tutu simply looked at him, then turned her gaze to the Wai river rushing past their log seat.

Coconut Man went inside himself and looked. He watched his dream again and found it sound. He felt the terror and heat of being in Pele's presence, her gratitude and fondness toward him. He smelled the fragrant blossoms in his mother's hair, the joy at the once captive spirits' release.

"*Ae*," he said in assent.

"So," Tutu continued as if there had not been a break in the conversation, "when you are regaling the men in the eating *hale* with your prowess, it will be how you wove the biggest basket, or some such tale, and not of meeting your Auntie Pele and your goddess mother, Uli."

Coconut Man had not thought of it quite that way before. He sometimes wondered what was in his head. *Yes, I was kidnapped by a sorcerer and Night Marchers tried to throw me into the volcano, but that was all right because I helped Madam Pele, who is my auntie by the way, so she and I are friends. Oh, and my mother is her sister, a goddess.*

Now he had no stories. "I understand, but what do I tell them?"

"I do not care. I care only that you do NOT tell them what happened." She patted his thigh with her warm brown hand and then used him to stand. "We will have more conversation later. I have much more to share with you. And we must continue your training. But for now, you have a young lady who needs you, too. As well as a noisy little boy who has done nothing all week but pine for his friend." She shuffled toward the village. She looked tired to Coconut Man. Perhaps she had been hard at work for him from here. He didn't know and probably never would.

"Kaleo managed to do no chores, either," she called back.

Coconut Man smiled and stood, ready to return to the village and those who wanted a story. He would have to come up with something. He turned to follow Tutu and saw Lele standing in a shaft of light on the trail. She looked beautiful, luminous and welcoming.

When he had left, their relationship was just beginning. They had been friends of a sort, through her son, but she and he . . . well, that had not been established. He definitely felt stirrings for her, but his nature combined with his nomadic life kept him from forming permanent bonds. With anyone. Since he had come to this village and seen a full turning of the seasons and celebrations, he had allowed himself to become part of the village. It had not been intentional, since as Tutu pointed out, he did not know how. It had seemed right and had flowed within and without him.

Now, seeing her in the light from the clearing, he felt his heart would burst. Her face said she felt the same. He rushed to her and they pressed foreheads, exchanging breath, but even this custom held more. He was aware of her body pressed to his, her strong arms crept around him and he held her tightly. Eyes closed, he simply felt her heart beat and reveled in the nearness of one he cared for so deeply.

"Hey!" Kaleo shouted. "Me, too!" He had found them. They broke apart and Coconut Man picked him up to join in the hug.

"You are heavy now," Coconut Man said.

"Or you are weak," Kaleo shouted. Everything was shouted, it seemed to Coconut Man. It had not been that many journeys of La that he had been absent this village, but Kaleo did seem bigger and stronger. Or, perhaps the small one was correct, that he had weakened from his ordeal on the lava. That was entirely possible.

Lele laughed, but her grasp of him did not lessen, so he felt strong enough. The three of them slowly wandered back to the main village. Coconut Man wondered if this is what a family would be like. It was a grand thought. He smiled at her, a promise they would meet later and her returning smile agreed. Lele parted ways saying she had tasks to do calling, "And Kaleo, your excuse for not working is over, so you must attend your chores as well." He grumbled but obeyed.

Coconut Man headed to the men's eating *hale*, with still no idea what tales to spin.

"Well, my son," said Uli's voice in his head, "we have had such an adventure, haven't we? And what will you name your own son next year?"

"Yes, nephew," said Pele. "I hope you continue to honor me."

"Coconut Man!" Tutu scolded. "Must I always remind you to stay with your tasks at hand? How will I continue your training if you are no more focused than the birds in the trees? I have much to teach and not much time to do it before . . ."

Coconut Man was so startled by all the voices that he tripped into the doorway of the men's eating *hale* and only caught himself on a support pole, entangled in the *pili* grass curtain. A spectacular entrance that cut short Tutu's words and perhaps a warning? *What did she say? And a baby next year?* It was all so much to take in. The men in the *hale* erupted in warm laughter, and for a moment,

Coconut Man stopped worrying about the future but just for a moment.

The End

Glossary–many Hawaiian words have more than one meaning. I chose the one which best applies to the story.

ahupua`a	land division from mountains to sea
aka	the essence spiritual; shadow, spirit
`aumakua	ancestral spirit
hale	house, home
kahuna	expert practitioner, priest,
kahuna 'ana'ana	witch, sorcerer
kāhuna	plural
kamali'i	children
keiki	child
kupuna	grandparent; ancestor
lo'lo'	idiot
mahalo	thank you
malo	loincloth
mana	authority, power
mele	chant, song
'ohana	family; clan
pī kai	to sprinkle water
pule	prayer; to pray, worship

On the Journey

Coconut Man	the basket weaver
Tutu	Coconut Man's teacher, a kahuna
Lele	a kapa (cloth) maker and love interest
Kaleo	Lele's son, a loud, happy boy
Moho	headman
Kula	aggressive villager
Nāwai	villager
Liloa	helpful villager
'Oloa	villager who disappears
Pua	woman who confides in Coconut Man
Kaiki	warrior and her husband
Hiwahiwa	their daughter
Lehua	village woman
Ana	healer kahuna

Gods and Goddesses

Kapo	goddess of poison and sorcery
La	the sun god
Namaka-o-Kahai	sister to Pele, ocean goddess
Pele	volcano goddess with a fiery temper
Uli	goddess of sorcery and resuscitation, restored life and health

References

Pukui, Mary Kawena (1972). *Nānā I Ke Kumu (Look to the Source) Vol. I.* Honolulu, Hawaii: Hui Hānai.

Pukui, Mary Kawena (1972). *Nānā I Ke Kumu (Look to the Source) Vol. II.* Honolulu, Hawaii: Hui Hānai.

Kamakau, S. M., (1964). *Ka Po'e Kahiko (The People of Old).* Honolulu: Bishop Museum Press.

Kamakau, S. M., (1976). *Na Hana a ka Po'e Kahiko (The Works of the People of Old).* Honolulu: Bishop Museum Press.

Curtis, Caroline, (1998). *Stories of Life in Old Hawai'i,* Honolulu, Kamehameha Schools Press.

Sohemer, S.H., (1993). *Plants and Flowers of Hawai'i,* Honolulu, University of Hawai'i Press.

Compiled by the Staff of Kamehameha Schools, (1994). *Life in Early Hawai'i – The Ahupua'a,* Honolulu, Kamehameha Schools Press.

Cunningham, Scott, (2000). *Hawai'ian Magic and Spirituality,* St. Paul, Llewellyn Publications.

Judd, Henry P, Pukui, Mary Kawena, Stokes, John F.G. (2004) *Handy Hawaiian Dictionary,* Honolulu, Mutual Publishing

Victoria Heckman's first *Hawai'i mystery series* features officer Katrina Ogden, K.O., of the Honolulu Police Department. Her second series, *Coconut Man mysteries of Ancient Hawai'i* begins with *Kapu-Sacred*. Her third mystery series (*Burn Out & Wet Work)* starring animal communicator Elizabeth Murphy is set on California's Central Coast. Stand alone mystery, *Pearl Harbor Blues,* begins on Dec. 7, 1941 and uncovers a dynasty of corporate intrigue. *K.O.'d at Banzai Pipeline* sends her to the big surf contests of O'ahu's North Shore (Jan.2016) She is also the author of over 75 short stories and articles and the editor of seven anthologies. She is a member of Sisters in Crime-Central Coast Chapter. Visit her website www.victoriaheckman.com or find her on Facebook, Twitter & Instagram.